MADDIE MAKES A MOVIE

SONIA GARRETT

For Rich,
Live, love and laugh.

THE BEST DAYS OF OUR LIVES?

"The first day of school is such a waste of time!" I shout over the hum of my remote control skateboard. "I could start back tomorrow and won't miss a thing, honest!"

"Oh, what a beautiful morning!" Dad sings at the top of his voice.

"Dad, are you listening to me? Why don't you answer when you know I'm making sense?" I say. "And no singing in public!"

I look over my shoulder to see him propelling his long board forward with all his might.

"Morning Mrs. Green," he calls out cheerily to the 'witch' who lives on the corner. She stands in her garden every year, watching us kids going to school at the end of the summer. It's some kind of sadistic ritual, seeing us all heading to our doom. She gives us sour looks, and snaps at us, if we walk on her grass or call to our friends, then says inordinately dull stuff to our parents like "Hasn't she grown" and "Ah, school days, the best days of your life."

She looks me up and down. Her lips and brows purse together. *What doesn't she like this time?* The black leggings, 'come over to the dark side' T-shirt and multi-coloured runners I have on are all practical. I can run, swing upside down and cartwheel in them. I still intend to enjoy recess even if I'm heading into grade five. But I don't want to look like a boy, so I've added mismatched socks and a pink tutu. Perhaps the pink streak in my long, curly hair or the black nails and fingerless gloves are going a little too far. I scowl at her and she looks as if she has just eaten a lemon.

Dad's suddenly beside me, tapping on my helmet "Wakey, wakey, Maddie. Race you to the school gate."

How did he catch up to me on that old thing? I press the trigger in my hand and accelerate around the corner.

He has the advantage travelling down the hill, but there's still the final straight to the gate. As we round the bend he's in the lead. He zigzags close to the cars, and I count three squeals as drivers open their doors without checking in their mirrors. I come up on the outside and race to the finish line. I bring the board to a halt just by the gate, jump up and hit the school sign with both hands then turn to high-five my dad.

He grins and has a gooey look in his eyes. *Oh no! He's going to give me a hug, or worse, a kiss, here in public.*

"Bye, Dad," I say firmly.

"So long, farewell, auf Wiedersehen, adieu; adieu, adieu to you and you and you..." Dad sings, blowing kisses in time with the music.

"Dad," I growl, giving him my best 'not here' look. "I'll make my own way home." Then turn swiftly, pick up my board and walk into school.

Parents can have such problems letting go. It's best to keep the goodbye short or they'll suffer all day without us. I'm ten and Mom and Dad still insist on taking me to school. At least I get to come home by myself and don't have to be cooped up in a car morning and afternoon like most kids.

"Maddie! That was cool," Ben Granger, a kid in grade

four who lives across the road from me, calls out as he climbs from his SUV.

"We saw the whole race!" his younger brother, Sam, yells. "Mom says it's 'irresportable.'"

"Irresponsible," Ben corrects.

"But I think it's awesome!" Sam continues.

"Where did you get it?" Ben asks, pointing to my skateboard.

"It was made for the movie Dad was filming over the summer, and I got to keep it when they were done," I say proudly.

"Lucky! How does it work?" Ben asks.

Some kids have gathered around my new electric skateboard. I place the board carefully on the playground, kneel next to it and show the enthusiastic crowd how the remote moves the board forward and backward. "It's just like an ordinary skateboard but with a motor that's controlled with this..."

"Give me a go!" Sam screeches, reaching out to grab the remote. I close my fist quickly, pulling the control mechanism into my chest and pressing the trigger by mistake. The board shoots across the playground, up the ramp, does a 360 degree, mid-air twist and lands with a CRASH right in the side of a metal garbage can outside the open office window.

Mrs. McIntyre's wrinkled face appears, ready to challenge the child who dares disturb her work. "Madeleine Moore, I might have guessed," she moans out the open window, shaking her head and turning her back on the playground.

First Mrs. Green, now Mrs. McIntyre. That's adult 'look' number two today and the bell hasn't even gone. What work does she do in a school office anyway? Answers the phone, puts on Band-Aids and sharpens pencils all day. Does she expect silence? Come on! This is an elementary school.

"Sorry," Sam squeaks. He looks at me with his big brown eyes. I can't stay angry with him. He didn't mean to destroy the best gift I have ever been given from a film set.

I feel sick, wondering if the board'll still work. No one moves. I'm going to have to be the one who checks the damage. I step forward, pick it up and spin the wheels one at a time. One, two, three wheels spin freely, but the last one sticks. I place my fingers gently on it and move the wide, black tire back and forth until I hear a click. Then with a twist of my wrist the final wheel turns and I let out a huge sigh of relief. The board appears to still be in one piece. Carefully, I place it on the asphalt. "Oh, please work," I pray under my breath. Stepping onto the platform, I balance my feet and press the trigger. The engine hums, the wheels move and I zoom across the playground, around the corner and head to the undercover area away from the prying eyes of parents, office workers and teachers.

"Oh no! Enemy approaching from the right," I mutter in mock horror. Raquel Roberts strides out of the shadow.

Her long black hair swings and moves as one, like Pocahontas or Mulan. Perhaps she's not real. Her designer clothes fit perfectly and she's grown over the summer. I can't believe it. She actually comes up to the shoulders of her constant companions, the bland, blonde One Direction twins, Sunshine and Raine Finkel. *No, wait, she hasn't grown. She's wearing heels. Runners with heels! How ridiculous!*

I skid to a halt in front of my enemies, kicking dust and stones in their direction.

"You're not allowed to ride in the school playground. And look what you've done to my new clothes," Raquel says, placing her hands on her hips.

Sunshine and Raine race to their leader and help to dust her down. I pretend I haven't heard her, but bend down, pick up my new board, place it under my arm and walk away. It's hard to believe that Sunshine and I were best friends in preschool. We played Princesses and dressed in pink all the time. I look at her pastel sweater covered with fairies and sequins. *I guess she still likes that stuff.* At least these days Raine doesn't cry all the time. She never used to stop bawling when I played with her twin.

In the distance, I see my best friend, Leila Choudhury, walking across the playing field with her mother. I have missed my BF so much. We only managed to FaceTime once in the whole time I was away with the film crew and since I've been home she has been 'busy.'

"Leila!" I shout, running towards her and get 'look' number three. I don't think Mrs. Choudhury likes me but my mom says, "we bring out the best in each other," whatever that means.

"Good morning, Madeleine," Mrs. Choudhury says. "Did you have a good summer?"

"Yes, thank you, Mrs. Choudhury. And yourself?" I say as politely as I can. Leila laughs and grabs my free arm as we hear the bell ring. I blush. I didn't mean to sound so formal. Leila's mom just makes me feel so awkward. She's the only person I know who actually speaks in full sentences. My mom says it's because she learnt English as an adult, but I've tried to learn French and I struggle to remember single words. I never even get to sentences.

"Leila, be a good girl and make sure you work hard," Mrs. Choudhury calls after us as we head towards the door.

And then I see them. There, in the far corner of the undercover area, is a huge pile of empty cardboard boxes. They're just sitting there, waiting to be used.

"Brilliant!" I shout.

Leila looks at me quizzically. "What?"

"I have an idea," I reply, smiling broadly.

School may not be so bad after all.

2

THE FALL SOCIETY

I'm the first one out at recess. Leila's close behind me, trying to put on a jacket.

"Mom says that I have to wear this. She doesn't want me to catch a cold," Leila shouts after me.

"You don't get colds from the cold," I say. "You can get hypothermia and that can kill you but..." I stop mid-sentence when I see the boxes. No one has cleared them during the morning. They are sitting in the corner of the undercover area, just like the pile in the corner of my dad's storeroom at work. Brilliant!

"Grab a box and take it to the far side of the bike shed," I shout.

"Why?" Leila asks.

"I'll explain when we get them there," I answer, lifting up three or four boxes. They are bigger than they look. I hold one end and let the other rest on the ground. I look over my shoulder. Not an adult in sight. It's safe to carry on. Leila has balanced a box on her head. It looks like a giant sombrero.

"La cucaracha, la cucaracha, ya no puede caminar," I sing as I half carry and half drag my load across the basketball court, toward the climbing frames.

"Bonjour, Madeleine. What are you doing?" Mme Perdu, our duty aid, calls out in her sing-songy voice.

"Recycling," I chirp back with my best innocent look on my face.

"Very good, very good," she replies taking out her phone and sitting in the sunshine with her back to us.

"Awesome!" I say under my breath. "Life just gets better and better."

Mme Perdu is the best duty aid we have. She's young, pretty and pays no attention to us kids. Last year I taught loads of kids how to fight in films while she watched the Soccer World Cup. It was the perfect time to set up a Fight Club, until we got caught.

I can feel one of the boxes sliding out of my hands as I walk, so I hook my toes underneath the pile and sorta hobble along. Reaching the far side of the climbing frames, I look over my shoulder. I still have to get across the soccer field and past the goal posts to where the trees, bushes and rusty metal shed will hide our new secret society. Pausing for a second to catch my breath, I can see a long dusty trail where my foot has dragged along the ground.

"Hey, Maddie!" Ben calls. "Can I help?"

"Grab the bottom of these boxes," I holler with relief. "I have an idea."

"What's the plan?" Ben asks.

"Wait and see." I drop the boxes out of sight behind the small shack that has two bikes and an old wheel still locked to a rack with a rusty chain. I add Leila's on top and look at the tiny pile. "We'll need way more than this."

I turn and run around the soccer field to avoid a group of boys who are fighting over who will be on which team. Leila and Ben are close behind me. I'm on a mission. We run past the climbing frames and spot Sam and his BF, Zack Miller.

"Sam, do you want to help?" I call.

"Maddie has an idea!" Ben adds.

"Cool!" Sam replies, running to join us.

There are five children carrying boxes on our next trip across the playground and eight for the one after that. *We'll get them all there in no time.* Then, BAM! A soccer ball slams against the box I'm carrying. The noise makes me jump and the box falls to the ground.

"Have you seen the processing power of these new computers?" Ivan Vladivenski asks, pointing at the box lying on the soccer field. "My dad was the head of the committee that chose them. They're the best."

"Of course they are," I say through gritted teeth.

Ivan is in my class and thinks he's the best at everything. He's always telling us he's the best hockey player, the best at Minecraft and Super Mario, and the best looking.

"Ivan, I don't care what was in these boxes," I pant with frustration and the effort of carrying the boxes to their new home. "Either help or buzz off!"

"Ooooo!" he laughs, running over to Leila and flicking the box off her head. He then turns his back on us and calls to the soccer players, "Three goals for us; zero for you. We are the champions!"

"Just ignore him," Leila says. "Or he'll keep bugging us."

We pick up our loads and continue moving and piling up boxes.

On our final trip back to the school building, I hear Raquel's voice echo around the concrete. I really don't want to deal with her nonsense right now.

"Put them back! They're ours! That's where the One Direction Fan Club meets," Raquel says with the twins nodding their heads just behind her.

"Not anymore," I laugh as I pick up one of the last few boxes.

Raquel stamps her foot in frustration and flicks her hair as she turns away from me. "Oh! Did you hear that?" she cries to her friends. "I'm telling!"

"I'm telling, I'm telling," I copy and leave Sunshine and Raine trying to comfort Raquel.

Finally, the last box has been put on the pile. We've done it. All the boxes are here. It hasn't rained. No one stopped us and I have a group of eager kids, all looking at me. My idea is working, tucked out of sight behind the almost unused bike shed. Strictly speaking, we shouldn't be here during the school day but what a waste! I look at all the excited faces. It's time to start.

"Whenever my dad jumps out of a window, falls from a roof or leaps from a tree, he lands in a box rig, a pile of empty cardboard boxes and never hurts himself... well hardly ever. I've helped build the rigs all summer and now I'm going to teach you," I say, striking a dramatic ringleader pose. "Welcome to the High Fall Society!

"Leila, you can be the first guard. If Mme Perdu looks up from her phone and turns towards us, shout 'I'm it!' and we'll all pretend to play tag."

Leila takes her post at the corner, looking across the soccer field. The rest of us quickly get to work folding the boxes and piling them up against the metal wall. The landing platform is soon ready.

"Now, watch me."

I climb to the roof of the shed, keeping my body low and out of sight. I crawl to the edge. It seems further down than I thought it would be. I look around. Mme Perdu's back is towards us with her head down. She's busy texting. Perfect. I stand, move to the edge and look down to the waiting faces then to the boxes. They look so far away. My heart's pounding in my chest. *Are there enough boxes? Perhaps the rig should be higher or wider?* I have to do this now. My stomach is jittery. My legs feel weak. *Three, two, one...jump.*

A huge cheer goes up and Leila shouts, "I'm it!" Children run around whilst I climb out of the half collapsed, slightly crumpled heap of boxes. I'm unhurt. The rig has worked and Mme Perdu only glances in our direction then goes back to her phone.

We pile up the boxes again, and one after another we leap into the rig that is getting smaller as recess goes on. Finally, everyone who wants a turn has had one and I can demonstrate the next move. I think of a challenge as I get to the top.

"Now, that was the standing jump. Next we have the running leap," I say while walking backward. I don't even check to see who's watching.

"Three, two, one...action!" I call, taking two running steps forward and launching myself into the air.

Mid-air, I hear a tangle of voices.

Mme Perdu screams.

"Stop!" Leila shouts.

Children run away screaming and laughing.

But over all the noise I hear Mr. Richardson's voice boom, "Madeleine Moore!" Then I land with a thud, close my eyes and lie very still.

For a second I wonder if I can pretend the boxes have swallowed me whole or that the school ghost forced me to jump. I look up. Raquel, Sunshine and Raine are standing just behind our tall, athletic principal. He's wearing a mauve, crisply ironed shirt and a long tie with a funky design. He would look like a catalogue model if he smiled, but he's not smiling. This isn't a good sign.

"Madeleine Moore, what do you think you are doing?" my principal questions. I don't think I should answer this just yet so I start to untangle myself from my cardboard crash mat.

That's when I realize there's no dignified way to get down from a box rig. Every time I move, one of my arms or legs disappears into another hole.

"I told you she was doing something dangerous," Raquel says, looking up into our principal's face, batting her eyelids and swaying her shoulders from side to side.

"Thank you Raquel. You did the right thing. There might have been a serious accident if you hadn't come to report this," Mr. Richardson replies slowly and clearly. "Mme Perdu, please make sure these children clear up this mess immediately."

I go to help, but I'm stopped in my tracks. "Not you Madeleine. You can wait by my office," Mr. Richardson says.

Everyone in the playground is very still, and it feels as if a hundred eyes are following me. *Has someone hit the pause button?* I turn and walk towards the blue-grey building.

My heart is thumping so loudly it's like a drummer counting in a band. In my head I can hear my dad's voice singing, "There May Be Trouble Ahead."

It's time to face the music.

3

THE PRINCIPAL'S OFFICE

Mom enters the school office looking stressed and dishevelled. Dad's close behind her. They both look at me, shaking their heads slowly. They made it to school in record time. They must have brought the car. I wish they'd taken their time and walked. Mom's always calmer after a walk, and there'd be no chance of Dad getting another speeding ticket.

They're here now and this is way too public for me to try to explain what happened. The next few minutes of my life won't be fun. I wonder how I'm going to be punished. No screen time, litter duty, grounded, sorting lost and found, cleaning Dad's truck with my tongue...

Mrs. McIntyre looks at me with her wrinkled brow then knocks on Mr. Richardson's door.

"Come in," Mr. Richardson calls.

Mrs. McIntyre pushes open the pale, wooden door

and we're ushered inside. There are three chairs facing the principal's desk.

"Mr. and Mrs. Moore, thank you for coming," Mr. Richardson says. "When there's a serious breach of safety on school premises, it's vital that parents and teachers work together to re-establish acceptable behaviours."

I sink down in the middle chair with Mom and Dad on either side. Mr. Richardson continues to talk as he returns to his desk, sits down and places his hand on a fat, brown file with my name written on it, which sits in the centre of the desk. There's a copy of the school's Code of Conduct resting on it. I know it well. I had to copy it out ten times last year and have already heard it read out over the PA this morning.

I look around the office to see if there've been any changes. There are several large piles of paper, stacked neatly around the wooden desk, and some photo frames, sitting to the...I look down at my hands and imagine which hand I would use to hold a pencil. *I write with my right hand so they are to the right.* Well, to my right. That means they are to his left. Now if I stood on my head, they would be on my left and on Mr. Richardson's left but we would still be looking at them from different directions. *Why are left and right so complicated!*

I have no idea why he has all these papers anyway. Are they his work for today or for the whole week? Does he have to take unfinished work home and finish it for homework? And who are the children in the photos? They must be his.

Imagine having a principal for a father. Yuck! Just think of the lectures you would get every time you did something wrong.

My eyes drift to a newly framed poster on the wall with a picture of a hammer hitting a screw. "To a hammer everything is a nail" is written in fancy writing. *What the heck is that meant to be about? And are Mom and Dad listening?* I look to one side. Mom is looking at Mr. Richardson and quietly nodding her head. On my other side, Dad is sitting very still but his eyes are darting around the room. *Maybe he's looking for an escape route. We could both smash through the window and run for our lives, like Harry and Hermione escaping from Lord Voldemort.* It seems like a better idea than just sitting and listening as Mr. Richardson goes on and on about "expected behaviours" and "compromising physical well-being."

I slide forward in my seat. My toes can reach the floor. I've grown since I last sat here. I try to listen but my eyes drift back to the window. The wind has picked up. There is some movement in the low branches and bushes outside. Well, it's either the wind or a bear rummaging around as he fattens up for winter. I wonder what would happen if I shout, "Bear!"

My thoughts are interrupted when Mrs. McIntyre knocks, enters the room and hands the principal a typed Incident Report.

Mr. Richardson opens my file and flicks through the

pages. I look upside down at the tiny school photos of myself stapled inside. I've really changed over the years. I looked really cute when I started school but oh, the bangs of grade three. *How embarrassing! They were a big mistake!*

He carefully places today's typed sheet of paper into the folder. Then he holds all the previous reports between his thumb and first two fingers.

"These unsafe activities have got to stop. Don't you agree Madeleine?" Mr. Richardson says. Then he pauses.

Help! All eyes are on me. *Am I meant to answer?* There's a long silence. Finally I mutter, "Err, sorry."

"You put your friends in danger. Maybe it's time for you to be with a new group of children. We could consider changing your classroom," my principal continues.

I look at him with panic in my eyes. *Move away from Leila! You can't do that to me! I'll do anything, anything at all but not that!*

"What you were doing wasn't safe," Mr. Richardson says with obvious frustration in his voice.

"No! I built the rig so no one would get hurt," I say defensively, looking up into Dad's blue eyes. I need someone on my side.

Dad puts his hand on my lap. Was there a slight smile at the corner of his mouth?

"Mr. and Mrs. Moore, in grade one your daughter broke her arm leaping from a swing," my principal reads from a report in the folder. "In grade two there was a cut to the forehead when your daughter was sword fighting with sticks..."

"It was a broad sword and it wasn't meant to touch the cardboard shield," I explain.

Mom gives me a look.

"In grade three you were excluded from Bike Safety Training because you were demonstrating how to crash bikes and fall off them. And last year you formed your very own Fight Club, here, on school premises."

When put together like this, my school record didn't sound good. I shift uncomfortably in my seat.

Mr. Richardson sighs, looks up from the folder and continues, "Can I ask how much screen time your daughter's allowed? I'm curious what computer games she plays and if she's watching age appropriate TV shows and movies?"

"Mr. Richardson," my mom says slowly and deliberately. "May I remind you Maddie's father works as a stuntman? What you have seen is creative play inspired by real life, not television."

Dad and I look at Mom. The room is silent for a moment. My principal gets up and starts looking through some papers in the recycling box. He pulls something out of the blue bin.

"Then can I suggest, your daughter's interests are used constructively, OUTSIDE SCHOOL HOURS," the principal says putting special emphasis on the last three words. He plunks the leaflet onto the table and pushes it towards me. "Perhaps she can show me how she can put your influence to good use."

"The Young Filmmaker of the Year Awards...Once Upon a Time" I read.

Wow. A film competition. Once Upon a Time. My brain starts whirring. A fairy tale theme. *Snow White?* No, I don't know any dwarfs. *Hansel and Gretel?* No, there's no way I'll be allowed all those sugary snacks. *Three Little Pigs?* Hmmm, how can I blow down houses? Using models perhaps. I don't use my dolls house anymore. An explosion would look amazing. I'll show him. I'll prove to Mr. Richardson I can do something great with my friends.

The meeting goes on. I'm going to have restrictions on the places where I can play. I have to stay in the climbing frame area and play near a duty aid for the rest of the week. The undercover area, basketball court, soccer field and forest areas are out of bounds. Is that it? *Not too bad, considering. Can I go?*

Finally, I get to write my name on a piece of paper entitled Behaviour Contract and we all stand up. The meeting is almost over.

"I hope this will be the last time I see you in here this year, Madeleine," Mr. Richardson concludes, shaking hands with Mom and Dad. "Show me how you can work constructively with your friends or the classroom change will be a real possibility."

I grab the leaflet about the competition and leave the office.

"I'll see you later," I say quickly, giving Mom and Dad a hug and racing back to class. I have to see Leila. *She'll help me!* I know she will. We have to get to work. We've got to win the Young Filmmaker of the Year award!

4

LIGHTS, CAMERA, ACTION

"*Little Red Riding Hood* should be easy enough," I say to Leila and Ben as we wander out into the warm September sunshine. "Leila, you can be Red. Ben, you'll be the camera operator and Red's father. I'll be the wolf.

"Skip down here," I continue, pointing to the concrete path that leads from the fire door to the soccer field below. "And I'll step out from behind that tree."

"But you have to play near the equipment," Leila reminds me.

"Fine. We can pretend that the firefighter's pole is a tree for the rest of this week and next week we can rehearse in the forest," I say.

I run down the steps, jump up onto the wood-chipped area around the climbing equipment and strike a casual stance with one hand behind my head, the other resting on my waist.

"Now, you come skipping up to me and I'll be here

waiting for you," I say, swinging one leg over the other and licking my lips.

"What do I do?" Ben asks, looking and sounding bored.

"You're the camera operator. Hold up your fingers like this," I say, showing him how to make a rectangle using his thumbs and forefingers.

"Close one eye and look at us as if this shape is the screen. If you are a long way from us, you see more background," I say.

I walk backward until I trip over the bottom step of the slide and bump into a tiny grade one girl I recognise from our 'buddy class.'

"Oh, sorry," I apologise.

Mme Perdu sits up tall and takes a sharp intake of breath. I smile and wave. She shakes her head, lowers her phone into her lap, but remains where she is. We both watch as the girl skips off to join her friends, apparently unconcerned about the incident. I breathe a sigh of relief and our duty aide lifts her phone back to her face.

"That's the wide shot," I say, returning to Ben. "Move in close and you can see the details on someone's face. This is a close-up."

I bend my knees and take small steps towards Leila until my hands are inches from her face. Ben copies me.

"Don't! It's embarrassing!" Leila says, shrinking away from our 'cameras.'

"Ha! They haven't got a hope of winning with a

camera shy leading lady!" Raquel sniggers and the twins copy.

We all turn around. How long have they been watching us?

"Looking for some ideas, Sneak?" I sneer.

"Why would we try any of your ideas? I've heard that you want to enter the Young Filmmaker of the Year," Raquel says, looking from Leila to Sunshine. "Give up now. My drama school wins first prize every year, and this year I'm going to be Snow White. You haven't got a hope.

"Leila, you could join Sunshine and Raine. Their names are on the wait list for my drama school. They're going to learn how to act properly as soon as there's a space. Or you could come and practice with a real star."

With that, Raquel flicks her long black hair over one shoulder then the other and walks away. Sunshine and Raine turn and follow their self-appointed leader, copying the flicks with their short blond braids. *They look ridiculous!*

I take three giant running steps across the wood chips onto the basketball court and shout after Raquel, "Where are they going to find seven kids who are shorter than you?"

"Madeleine!" Mme Perdu screeches. "Kind words, please! And you must play near the climbing frames or we'll both be in trouble."

"Argh! Now, we have to win," I say to Leila and Ben.

"Let's try the final battle between the wolf and Red's father."

"What battle?" Ben asks. "I thought the father came in, saw the wolf asleep, and chopped him open with an axe."

"Not in our version," I say, lying down on the ground. "You enter, calling for Red. I'll pretend to be asleep but there'll be a close-up on the wolf opening one eye, just like Smaug in *The Hobbit*. Then when you come close, the wolf will roll off the bed and grab something."

I roll over in slow motion and search for an object to fight with. "Perfect!" I say, spotting a long stick lying on the ground near a bush. I look around. Mme Perdu is smiling at something on her phone. The coast is clear. I quickly run out of the wood-chipped area, grab the stick, break it in two and jump back into my restricted play area. I hand one stick to Ben.

"This can be your axe and I'll use this half as Granny's walking stick," I explain.

"Now, raise your axe, as if you are going to kill me," I say, lying back down on the ground. "I'll roll over, pick up the walking stick and block your chop. Then you swing the axe at my feet, I'll jump over it, catch you off balance, knock the axe from your hand and force you against the wall."

We walk through the fight in slow motion until I have Ben pinned against the climbing wall with the stick at his neck. He is trying to push me away with all his might, but the wolf is too strong for him.

"Madeleine! Madeleine! What are you doing?" Mme Perdu shouts. "No sticks!"

"But we were only..." I reply.

"Madeleine! Non, non, non. No sticks! No fighting! No violence! Come and sit with me, right now or I'll lose my job. And you two; go and play somewhere else. Shoo, shoo, shoo. Off you go!" Mme Perdu's voice squeaks when she is really angry and the pitch is getting higher and higher so I let my shoulders slump in defeat and hold my stick out towards Ben. *Life is so unfair! We weren't hurting anyone! We were just rehearsing what could have been the best fight ever filmed!*

Ben takes the stick from my hand and I watch my friends just standing there, as I walk towards our duty aid. I sit down on the concrete step next to Mme Perdu, grit my teeth and bury my head in my hands, feeling frustration surging through my body. *How are we going to win the competition if we can't rehearse? And if I don't win, how can I show Mr. Richardson that I can work with my friends?*

I lift my head to see Leila and Ben walking towards the soccer field. Ben kicks a ball that has rolled towards him, drops the sticks on the ground and runs to join in the game. Leila sits down with her back to me. I can see her long black braid. It covers the whole of her spine and falls below the metal bench. I sit up and take a closer look.

Leila's hair is perfect! How could I have missed it? We're rehearsing the wrong story.

"Leila, with your long hair, we have to film *Rapunzel*," I say the next day as I push open the fire exit and head outside for recess. "I'll be the witch and Ben can be the prince."

"But you can't climb up my hair!"

"Don't worry. I know a way to make it work. My dad often hides safety wires inside his costume. Like the time he had to jump from a tree onto a carriage. He was wearing a harness under his costume with wires attached. There were guys lowering him down gently, so there was no way he could get hurt. I was on set for a whole day. It looked amazing," I explain.

"We'll braid your hair around some climbing rope and it'll look as if we're using your hair to climb the wall. But really I'll be using the rope." I say, but Leila doesn't seem to get it.

I grab Leila's hand and pull her to the climbing wall that's only a bit taller than we are. "Sit up on the platform and look unhappy, as if you've been locked in a tower all your life."

"Hey Ben! What kept you?" I say as Ben climbs up the metal spiral ladder, crosses the bridge over the monkey bars and jumps down to me.

"Now, I'll come along as the witch. Ben, you're the camera operator until you're needed as the prince."

"Witch? Prince?" Ben says.

"Are you ready? Camera! Action!" I shout.

Ben shrugs his shoulders and makes a rectangle with his fingers.

I hunch over and scrunch up my face. "Rapunzel! Rapunzel! Let down your hair!"

I grab the plastic footholds and reach the top in three easy strides. Leila's unbraided hair reaches well below the platform.

I gather all the long strands with my spare hand and divide them into three long, almost even sections.

"The outside strand comes to the middle, the outside strand comes to the middle," I say to myself as I weave Leila's hair around the rope. Some bits of hair fall out of the braid, but I just gather them back into my handiwork and continue until the remaining hair is too short to reach. I tie off the loose strands with a hair elastic and jump to the ground.

"I'll have to practice braiding," I admit, looking up at the tangled hair. "But it'll be okay for a test."

"Are you sure?" Leila asks.

She leans her head away from her body towards the hair-covered rope and holds onto the platform with her thin fingers poking through the red metal holes on the surface.

"Yeah, it's fine," I say. "Now, I've already said,

'Rapunzel, Rapunzel let down your hair.' So now I am going to climb the wall. Cameras rolling! Ready! Action!"

Ben holds up his fingers to make the screen. I reach with one hand and curl my fingers around the climbing rope. Place a foot on the wall. Then push off the ground, take a handful of hair, and push out and up with all my might.

The rope jerks away from the solid equipment frame and pulls Leila with it. Her legs swing out, kicking me in the face and sending me flying backward onto the wood chips. I land with a thud. The wind is knocked out of me.

Instinctively, I close my eyes for a split second and lie quite still. The side of my face aches, but I am sure there are no broken bones. Somewhere above me, Leila is screaming. I open one eye to see her legs kicking the air.

"Ah! Get me down! Get me down!" Leila screams with one hand around her hair, the other stuck in the holes of the platform, holding herself up.

"Zut alors!" Mme Perdu exclaims, running from her concrete seat.

"You, you, you!" she shouts at Ben. "Run and get some scissors!"

"No! You can't cut my hair!"

The sound of the bell drowns out Leila's voice. I jump up, grab her legs, and try to lift her back onto the platform.

"Just stay still," I shout, reaching for the hair tie and pulling it out. "I can undo this if you just stop wriggling."

A small crowd is gathering to watch. Out of the corner of my eye I see Raquel pushing her way to the front.

"You won't get your film made just hanging around," Raquel calls, as the quickly emptying playground echoes with a chorus of mocking laughter.

5

THE CRAZY THERMOMETER

By the time I eventually find our class in the computer room, my face throbs with blood rushing to my swollen and quickly blackening eye. My skin stings because of the ice pack that Mrs. McIntyre insists stays on for another ten minutes. My stomach feels like a churning mix of humiliation and shame, and my heart aches because my best friend won't speak to me. I look down the hallway. Leila is staring at the floor and shuffling towards the classroom.

The image of another Incident Report page being placed into my school record haunts me. I want to run away. I want to go home. I want to hide under my duvet and never come out. *No more big ideas. I will never tell anyone any of my ideas ever again.*

Slowly, I raise my hand to the doorknob and glance over to Leila. She turns her head. She is standing a few feet away from me. Her eyes are red and swollen. She runs her fingers through her matted hair. She stops and holds a short section in front of her face and starts crying again. I want to hug her and tell her it will be fine, but I don't believe life will ever be okay again.

Why did Mme Perdu use scissors? Why did we try Rapunzel? Why did I ever think that I could make a film? Why was I ever born?

I push the door open and step inside. Leila is close behind me. The whole class turns towards us, stares in disbelief for a second then erupts into peals of laughter. Morgan even falls off his chair, he's laughing so hard. Mr. Phillips, our teacher, holds his hand to his mouth, but I can see from his eyes that he is struggling not to join in with the laughter. *This is the worst day of my life!*

"Leila, come and sit with Sunshine. Maddie, you can share with Ivan. We're reviewing *Keyboard Ninja*. How many of you have finished exercises one to ten?" Mr. Phillips asks.

My class groans and slowly returns to their work.

"Do you want a turn?" Ivan asks.

"No, thanks," I reply as I take the ice pack away from my face. Mr. Phillips is marking our 'What can you remember?' math test. All around me are the familiar and somehow calming sounds of computer keyboards clicking and children whispering.

I've often wondered why Ivan chooses the computer in the back corner. Now, I can see why. He has flicked over to Khan Academy and is moving geometric shapes around the screen.

"What are you doing?" I ask.

"Shhh! If Mr. Phillips sees me, I'm dead meat," he says.

I shrug my shoulders and look away. Notes are being passed from friend to friend, which gives me an idea. I tear off a scrap of paper from the print-out sitting on the desk and grab a pencil. 'Leila, I am SOOOOO sorry. You are my BFF. Please forgive me. Maddie.' When I've finished writing the note, I cover the page in hearts, fold the paper three times and write 'Leila' on the outside. I pass it along the line, watching its progress until it reaches my best friend. *Will she take it? Is she my BFF or ex-BFF?*

Leila is looking at the computer screen and hitting the letters on the keyboard in the order they appear on the fish swimming across her monitor. Sunshine taps her on the shoulder and shows her my note. Leila takes it, looks towards me, looks away without smiling and puts the note, unread, in her pocket.

This day cannot get worse. I turn to the screen. Ivan has created a picture of a prince with a round head, oval body and triangles for a crown. The figure moves stiffly across the screen until a tower comes into view. A braid, made from tiny triangles, falls down the side of the tower. *My humiliation is complete.* Ivan can animate *Rapunzel* better than I can film it.

Ivan's prince reaches up with his fat, oval-shaped

arms. Clouds of lines and circles shoot from his bottom. The figure jumps off the ground. There's another puff of gas, followed by another jump and the prince rises up the side of the tower using fart power.

I burst out laughing.

"Maddie, I fail to see what could be that funny in the computer room. Please let Ivan concentrate on his work," Mr. Phillips comments, lifting his head only briefly from his marking.

"Yes, let me 'concentrate on my work,'" Ivan copies, looking pleased with himself.

My face goes red and hot. Everyone in the class looks at me. Raquel holds her finger to the side of her head and circles her temple. Sunshine and Raine cover their mouths to stifle their giggles. I look to Leila for some support, but her eyes stay focused on the computer screen.

"Don't let them worry you," Ivan says. "When I go to Computer Club my soccer friends call me a nerd. When I play hockey, the geeks call me a jock. But I am just me. I like this kind of stuff," he admits, nodding his head in the direction of the cartoon.

"Look! You gave me this idea." Ivan reaches into his pocket and pulls out a crumpled application for the film competition. "Have you seen all the prizes you can win?"

It takes me a couple of seconds to understand what I am looking at. *Surely Ivan isn't planning to enter the same competition as I am. I mean, that I was going to enter.*

Come on, Maddie. Loads of kids will be entering. It'll be almost impossible to impress Mr. Richardson this way. What chance have I got of winning anyway? I look to where he's pointing.

"The winner gets to go on a week-long camp at a real film school. Plus there are cameras, editing packages, a master-class on animation and a term of classes at All Action Inc to be won," Ivan reads.

"I know," I say angrily.

It's really very simple! I want to be the filmmaker in this class and Raquel is my rival. That's the way it works! I know it's crazy, but I don't need more competition. Ivan, should stick to the Science Fair and leave this one to me. I have way more ideas than a silly shape figure, climbing a wall, using fart power.

Although, it did make me laugh... Even Leila would laugh if she saw it. Oh please laugh, Leila, or at least smile. If you smile, I'll know we'll be friends again soon.

I look over to Leila. Sunshine passes her a note. She opens it and looks towards me. When she sees I'm looking at her she blushes and quickly folds the note.

"Let me see!" I mouth silently, beckoning furiously with my hand.

Leila shakes her head.

"Come on!" I say with my lips, putting on my best pleading face.

Leila takes the note in her hand and throws it at me. She is definitely still mad at me. Leila never throws anything. She is really bad at throwing, and she would never want to get caught breaking school rules. The note lands on the floor a little way from my feet. I drop to my hands and knees to get it.

Slowly, I open the paper, sitting right there on the floor. There is a thermometer drawn on the paper with the title, 'CRAZy Thermometer.' Raquel, Sunshine, Raine and Leila's names are all written against the normal mark, and my name is bursting out of the top in enormous bubble writing. I want to cry. I can hear some muffled laughter. I know where it's coming from, but I can't look. If my enemy sees me crying she'll know she's won. I should go back to my chair, but some strange weight seems to be resting on my shoulders and I can't move.

"Ivan, I can't see *Keyboard Ninja* on your screen," Mr. Phillips says, standing right behind us.

Ivan jumps and tries to hide the crumpled application under the worksheet on his desk.

"I'll have that, Mr. Vladivenski," Mr. Phillips says, holding out his hand.

Ivan holds out the form then looks at me. I look up into my teacher's eyes.

"Maddie, go back to your seat," he says sternly.

I quickly put my hand, with the note in it, behind my back and stand up.

"And I'll have the piece of paper you are trying to hide from me," Mr. Phillips continues.

I hand it over and back into my chair. My eyes stay focused on our teacher. He looks at the film application and the CRAZy Thermometer, nods his head then studies them both again.

"Hmmm," he says slowly.

Ivan clicks away at the keyboard. *How can he work so fast?* Khan Academy disappears and *Keyboard Ninja* reappears. He is about to press start but suddenly seems to notice that no one else is working. Everyone's eyes are facing the front of the room. *Wow, the computer room is weird when it is silent.*

"Well, for the first time today, I seem to have everyone's attention," Mr. Phillips says. "This seems to be about the film competition I keep hearing about. Ivan, I am guessing you want to win Cinema Prime 4D. It's about the only thing your dad didn't manage to buy for the school. Or maybe even the film-editing course. What about you Maddie?"

I shrug my shoulders and wonder what my teacher is getting at. Everyone is looking from us to Mr. Phillips like it's a tennis match. I hold my breath and wonder what will happen next. Will I be sent back to Mr. Richardson's office? Twice in one day would be a personal record.

"Mme Perdu told me about your *Little Red Riding Hood* fight, and your class mates have told me all about the technical problems with Rapunzel's hair. Which of the prizes do you want to win?" Mr. Phillips asks.

I keep my eyes focused on some dirt on the floor.

"Having dreams is healthy," Mr. Phillips continues. "You have both set yourself a goal. A hard one to achieve and you are working towards it. Ivan, you can't use class time to work on your entry. Maddie, you should want everyone to survive this project so they can go on to the next."

Everyone laughs at this and I feel the blood rushing to my face. I look at Ivan. We are being talked about together. *Ergh! This is weird! What have we got in common? NOTHING!*

"You know," Mr. Phillips resumes. "Having dreams and setting goals for yourself isn't a bad thing. I know many of you dream of having a smartphone, but I am old enough to remember when there were no smartphones. Then a man called Steve Jobs came along and refused to accept that the cell phones of the day were the best they could be. He made happen what other people thought was impossible. He even said something like, 'The people who are crazy enough to think they can change the world are the ones who do.' So if trying out ideas, entering competitions and taking a few risks is 'crazy,' then my wish for you is that you all burst out of the top of the Crazy Thermometer.

"But enough of my chatter. Maddie and Ivan, I'm proud of you and I hope you'll invite me to the award ceremony. If I were in this class, I would make friends with these two. They're going places.

"Now, who has finished this *Keyboard Ninja* work?" Mr. Phillips taps the whiteboard with the end of his red pen. "And Ivan, I think it's Maddie's turn on the computer."

The familiar sounds of the keyboards clicking and voices whispering return.

Ivan and I change places. I still can't believe we've been lumped together. I sit at the keyboard and press the start button. Frogs with letters on their backs jump onto logs on the screen. I hit the keys that go with the letters. Almost immediately my mind wanders. *Frogs, hmm, toads... Would* The Princess and the Toad *work? No, no more films. I can be normal. Just type. What does Mr. Phillips know about 'going places'? The only place I ever go is the principal's office to get another Incident Report.* The letter f appears on the next frog. I hit the 'f' key.

Then the letter 'a' appears. I know what to do. I type. F, a, f, r, f, a, f, r... but my mind begins to drift, *far, far away...* *Stop! There won't be a film! Yesterday's rehearsal was a disaster. Today's rehearsal was worse and there won't be one tomorrow. Leila hates me. And no matter what I do, Raquel will beat me.*

But just imagine if I actually won... Mr. Richardson will see what I can do, Mr. Phillips would be SO proud and I could go to All Action Inc. Dad told me they actually teach three different types of sword work, cloak and dagger fighting, hand-to-hand combat and horseback archery. How cool is that?!

"You may want to read this if you're not going to do any typing," Ivan whispers, passing me a scrap of paper. "Swap places."

Ivan takes my seat at the computer and I move to his chair. I hate sitting on warm plastic chairs, especially when a boy has been sitting there before me. I turn the folded piece of paper over in my hand. It's tiny. My thumb almost covers the note. 'Maddie' is written in Leila's beautiful, cursive handwriting. I look over towards her. She looks away from me and back to her computer.

I open the first fold and read, 'sorry.' I look towards her and she's smiling at her screen. I open the second fold and read, 'really, really sorry.' The third fold has a stick figure girl with curly hair and a giant cup with '1st' written on it. Under the next fold it says, 'Please let us be in your film.' When I open the final fold there is a long list of names. Leila's name is at the top with a smiley face drawn in a heart, then Summer has put her name with brackets after it saying '(I'll get Raine to be in it BUT DON'T TELL RAQUEL),' then Yan Yan, Stu, Ollie, Morgan... the list goes on and on until finally Ivan has added his name right at the bottom of the page.

"You're going to make the winning film. I know you are," Ivan says matter-of-factly.

6

CRASH TEST DUMMY

"Why is it that when you want it to be the weekend, every school day lasts forever, but when there's so much to do, Saturday comes around really quickly?" I wonder aloud, putting thick globs of chocolate spread onto a piece of toast.

"Hmm, that's a healthy breakfast," Mom comments sarcastically.

"Come on, a director needs loads of energy," I say, picking up the piece of toast in one hand and the hand-written script in the other.

"And when is this director going to clean hamster cages?" Mom questions.

"What? Not now, Mom. We haven't made the carriage for Cinderella yet and everyone arrives to start filming in a couple of hours."

"Tell me then, why did you bring the class pet home this weekend when you don't have time to look after your own hamster?" Mom asks, raising her eyebrows and staring at me.

"I need them both and I need you to be head of catering. Remember, Sunshine and Raine can't eat toffee, corn on the cob or popcorn because of their braces. Nothing from a pig for Leila and our prince is gluten intolerant but he probably won't come today because he has a hockey tournament and he can only be here if they do badly and get kicked out in the early rounds. And, believe me, we don't want that. Ivan is a nightmare when he doesn't win," I say without drawing breath.

Mom's about to say something but Dad comes into the kitchen doing a strange hop and a skip, singing, "Bring me sunshine, bring me rain." Mom laughs and gives him a kiss on his way to the coffee machine.

"Err! You two are gross! Don't you dare do that in front of my friends," I say.

"Don't worry, Princess. I'll be in the garage all day, keeping well away from the creative process," Dad says, puckering his lips and threatening to kiss me as well.

"Cut it out!" I say, ducking away from him.

"Well, good luck," Dad says. "And remember, when Plan A doesn't work, there's always Plan B."

Dad picks up his coffee thermos in one hand and grabs an apple in the other. He tosses the apple in the air, bounces it off his upper arm, and catches it again. Then he takes a huge bite out of the crisp juicy flesh and heads for the door.

What a cool trick!

I tuck my script under my arm, lean across the table, grab an apple from the fruit bowl, toss it into the air a couple of times and manage to catch it using only one hand. *Now there's just the bicep bounce.* I throw the apple back into the air and move my arm towards it. I miss the apple completely and it lands on the floor with a thud. *This is definitely harder than it looks.*

"Hey, Maddie!" Dad shouts from the front yard. "It looks as if the troops are arriving."

"On my way!" I reply, picking up the apple and tossing it back into the air. The apple meets my arm as it falls back to earth and I bat it so hard that it flies across the kitchen, bounces off the fridge, onto the counter and knocks over the pot with all the wooden spoons in it.

"Maddie! What are you doing?" Mom yells.

"Nothing," I reply.

I drop my script on the floor and quickly collect up all the kitchen stuff so I can shove it back into the pot. There are crumbs everywhere. I try to wipe them off the work surface, onto the floor with my sleeve.

"Just leave that," Mom says wearily.

"Thanks, Mom," I reply, gathering up all the rehearsal notes.

"Maddie!" Ben and Sam shout from outside. "Help!"

I look at the pages that are now crumpled, out of order and covered in chocolate. I dump them on the table. *We don't need this. I'll be like that famous director who works without a script. If it's good enough for Mike What's-his-name, it's good enough for me,* and I run out of the front door.

Outside, Ben and Sam are struggling across the widest section of our cul-de-sac. Their bikes are sticking out of an old shopping cart. The wheels are bouncing over the uneven road surface, making a loud clatter as metal bangs against metal.

"That's perfect!" I shout.

"Dad, can we use one of your rigging boxes to make the pumpkin?" I ask. "Sure. Help yourself," Dad replies, smiling at the three of us from his position, squatting on the garage floor next to his motorbike.

Ben, Sam and I grab a box between us, squeeze past the motorbike parts, oil can and tools, pick up a Sharpie from the workbench and head for the yard.

The grass is still damp and the air feels cool. We should have started filming weeks ago. *Why does it take grown-ups so long to get a group of kids together?* I look up. There are some light clouds in the sky. *Please, please, please don't rain on our carriage!* We lay the box down and I draw a large pumpkin shape on one side. We'll have to work fast so that the box doesn't get soggy.

Running back into the garage, I take an X-Acto knife out of the large red tool cabinet. Carefully pointing the sharp end towards the ground, I walk as fast as I can back to the boys.

"Start cutting out the pumpkin. I'll go and get some paint," I say.

A few minutes later, I return carrying an empty yogurt pot, some poster paints and three brushes.

"Yellow and red make orange," I say, taking the bottle of yellow in one hand and the red in the other and squeezing the paint into the pot. "Mix that up and start painting. I'm going to find something to attach the bikes to the cart."

I appear from the garage a few minutes later, carrying some bits of old fraying rope and some electrical ties. The pumpkin is burnt orange with streaks of yellow through it.

"That looks cool!" I say. "But you two will have to clean your hands before you become the footmen. Cinderella wasn't taken to the ball by servants covered in paint! You look like you're ready for Halloween.

"But hey, you've given me an idea! We can use my fake film blood and some tomato ketchup to make the end more dramatic. Cinderella can run from the castle, jump into the carriage, race away and have a huge crash just as the clock strikes twelve. The carriage, footmen, horses and ball gown will disappear and Cinderella will limp home wearing rags, covered with blood and mud. It'll look awesome!" I squeal.

Ben and Sam exchange looks as we lift the cardboard pumpkin and attach it to the cart with electrical cable ties.

Next, we turn our attention to the horses. Cardboard horse heads, ears and rope tails are all fixed onto the bikes.

When the parts of the carriage are complete, it's time to put it together. We tie ropes to the bike frames and the shopping cart handle. Stand back and admire our work.

"Come on!" I say. "It's time to test our creation."

Ben and Sam jump onto their bikes and start pedalling down the road. The cart bounces after them but stays more or less in a straight line.

"Turn around," I shout.

The boys pedal across the road and turn to come back. Our pumpkin follows, tips onto two wheels as it turns the corner, and lands on its side with a bump. Ben quickly slams on his brakes and puts his feet down on the road. Then he manages to catch Sam before he falls on top of him.

"That's okay!" I say, running over to the fallen carriage. "It just needs to be weighed down. I'll put on pads and we'll have another go."

Ben and I pick up the cart while Sam holds the bikes. Then I run into the mudroom, put on my skateboard knee and elbow pads, rollerblade wrist guards, horseback-riding back protector and ski helmet.

"When Cinders goes to the ball, we'll travel slowly, like a royal carriage," I explain, running back outside, placing first one leg then the other over the side of the metal basket. "But on the way home, you'll pull the pumpkin as fast as you can, we'll hear the clock striking twelve, the carriage'll disappear and Cinders'll be thrown onto the ground. It'll look fantastic!

"Ready?" I shout, holding tightly onto the sides. "Go!"

"You weigh a ton," Ben cries over his shoulder, as the bikes gradually move forward.

"Come on! Pedal harder! I don't want to be late for the ball!" I yell.

The bikes gain speed and my whole body vibrates. I take one hand off the side and wave, then the other hand comes up and I try to stand upright. I can feel my toes curling in my runners, trying to grip hold of something. I hold my breath. It's working.

"Okay, now let's speed up!" I scream.

Ben and Sam push with all their might. Their bikes speed up and the cart, with me in it, bounces behind them.

The rope between the bikes and Cinder's carriage loosens a little and then tightens with sudden jolts, throwing my body backward and forward like a roller coaster ride. "Yeehaw!" I screech, tightening my grip on the sides. "Faster! Faster!"

The boys push harder and the carriage gains speed.

"This part of the road goes downhill slightly. Perfect for when we're filming Cinderella heading home," I shout over the noise of the wheels rattling along the road.

"Car!" Ben hollers.

The two boys turn their bike handlebars and steer away from the oncoming car, as they have done many times before when playing on the road between our houses. But this time I realize that we don't know how to stop the carriage. The bikes come to a gentle stop. Ben and Sam place their feet onto the road. But I keep going.

The carriage sails past Ben's and Sam's horror-struck faces. The rope between us tightens, the front wheels of the cart brake suddenly, throwing me onto my knees while the back wheels continue with their journey. They skid around 180 degrees before the cart topples over and I tumble sideways onto a pile of freshly raked leaves.

"Hooligans!" Mrs. Green yells, running at us with garden shears in her hands. "Get off my grass!"

"Run!" I shout.

We quickly pick up the bikes from the ground and run back to my house, pushing Cinderella's carriage as fast as the rickety wheels and our laughter will allow.

The car that caused us to crash has stopped outside my house. Sunshine, Raine and Leila all get out. Leila runs to me wearing a long flowing Belle costume while the twins stand with their mouths wide open.

"Are you okay?" Leila asks, looking at me and then back to her mother's worried face.

"Madeleine, that was quite a fall. Did you hurt yourself?" Mrs. Choudhury asks.

"No, I'm fine," I reply. "Stunt performers wear all this padding so they are okay for filming. It's like being a crash test dummy."

"But you won't be trying that again, will you?" Mrs. Choudhury questions seriously.

I am going to tell her about the dramatic end to Cinders night at the palace but decide just to say no.

"And who is going to supervise you children today?" Mrs. Choudhury continues.

Leila looks worried and is trying to say something silently like "Don't say another word" without moving her lips. Her eyes are nearly popping out of her head. She is staring at me and clenching her jaw.

"Hey there!" Dad calls, walking out of the garage and wiping his oily hands on a filthy cloth. "You into the action already?"

"Just doing some tests while we're waiting for the cast to arrive," I explain.

"Isn't this great," Dad continues, turning to Leila's

mom. "Most parents are struggling to get their kids away from the screen and ours are out here, creating."

"I guess so," Mrs. Choudhury says, doubtfully.

"Come on," I say, before she can change her mind. "You guys won't believe what I have planned for today."

7

QUIET ON SET

"Cinderella!" Sunshine calls. "Bring me a ribbon!"

"Cut," I sigh, pressing the button to stop recording on my iPad. "That's not how it goes, Sunshine. You are supposed to say, 'Sweep the floor!' You have to say the same line every time."

For someone who gets straight As she can sure act dim.

"But I thought as Raine is brushing my hair, it would be nice to have a ribbon in it for the ball," Sunshine replies.

"You don't even know about the ball yet," I say. "This is a scene before the invitation is delivered!

"Raine, you are going to brush Sunshine's hair. Sunshine, you will call out, 'Cinders,' then I will step into the shot and you will say, 'Sweep the floor.'"

I look around for Ben. He and Sam are squatting on the driveway watching my Dad putting his motorbike back together.

"Ben," I call. "You need to be the camera operator."

Ben stands up reluctantly and wanders over to where we are filming. Sunshine is sitting on a garden bench in front of some rose bushes. Raine and Leila have their arms around Sunshine, comforting her.

"What's wrong now?" I ask, trying not to sound frustrated.

"I don't think I can do this without Raquel," Sunshine cries. "She's really good at this sort of thing and would tell me what I have to do."

I can't believe what I am hearing. I'm telling Sunshine what to do and she just isn't listening. How can she mention Raquel to me, here, in my own home? Right now she's probably filming her 'award winning entry' with her drama school while we're still working on the first scene.

Come on! There's got to be a way to do this! Then I remember all my dad's stories about difficult actors and how they become easy to work with if they are given just the right compliment.

"Sunshine, you're doing a great job," I lie. "We can hear every word you say and you... look great on the screen."

Sunshine looks up and smiles. "Really?"

"Really," I say. "Now please say, 'Cinders,' then I will step into the shot and you will say, 'Sweep the floor!'"

"But we're outside," Raine says, taking up her place behind Sunshine. "There isn't a floor."

"Okay," I reply. "Say, 'Cinders! Sweep the stairs!' or

'Cinders! Rake the leaves!' Anything you like but don't mention the ball!"

I turn my back to everyone. *Breathe, just breathe, calm down and breathe.* When I turn around, everyone looks ready. Sunshine is sitting on the bench, Raine is standing behind her, and Ben is holding the iPad with his finger near the record button. Leila and Sam are watching out of shot.

"Scene one, take eight," I say, smiling encouragingly at Sunshine. "Three, two, one, action."

Ben pushes the record button and Raine starts brushing Sunshine's hair. I smile and mouth Sunshine's line.

"Cinders!" Sunshine shouts, and I step closer to the bench.

"Cinders! Sweep the floor!" Sunshine says.

"Cut! Yes, yes, yes, you did it!" I shout, hugging Sunshine.

"Didn't we change the line?" Leila whispers in my ear.

"It doesn't matter," I reply. "We have our first scene in the can! That's film speak meaning it's finished."

"Anyone for a snack?" Mom calls, carrying a tray of apple slices, grapes and glasses of iced water.

We all crowd around the tray, grab a cup of water and some fruit. I bite into the apple and have an idea.

"Come with me everyone. We can film Cinder's

chores in the back yard. There are far better jobs you can ask me to do there," I say.

We walk around the side of the house, carrying our water glasses, fruit and props. Sam runs straight to the trampoline and starts bouncing. Ben looks at me with 'Can I have a go as well?' eyes.

"Sure. Have a go while I sort out the next shot," I say, looking up at the old apple tree.

"If you ask me to get you an apple," I explain to the twins. "We could film me climbing the tree and picking them. It would look way more exciting than sweeping, mopping or dusting."

"Oh, yes!" Sunshine squeals. "Cinderella! I'm hungry. Get me an apple."

"Yes! Perfect! Let's go for a take," I say, putting my water down on the table.

"Ben," I call. "We need you to operate the camera."

"We could be sitting here," Raine suggests, pointing to the small tiled garden table. "Painting our nails."

"Great idea," I say. "And I could be raking leaves, as if that was an order you've already given me."

I run inside and come back with a basket of nail polish and the shed key. Sunshine and Raine look through all the tiny glass bottles and start arguing about which colour they will paint onto their fingernails, while I open the shed and get the rake.

Much to my surprise, I come out of the shed to find

Ben filming, turning the camera between the twins and me.

"Cut!" I shout. "That's not the scene."

I explain what's going to happen to everyone and start raking the leaves into a pile.

"Silence on set," I call. "That's what they always say when they're making a real movie. And action!"

There are so many leaves under the tree that it's easy to make a big pile with two long strokes of the rake. *Please be getting this on camera, Ben!*

"Cinderella! I'm hungry. Get me an apple," Raine calls.

"Oh, yes, me too!" Sunshine says.

"Can't you get it yourself?" I reply, but the twins wave their newly polished purple glittery fingernails at me and give me a 'you have got to be joking' look they have learnt perfectly from Raquel.

I sigh, drop the rake, spit on my hands and rub them together so they are ready for climbing. The first part of the climb is the hardest. I put my arms around the lowest branch then walk my feet up the trunk. Once my body is almost horizontal, I throw one leg over the branch and turn myself over so that I am lying on my stomach with my legs dangling on either side. Then I place my feet on the branch behind me and inch my way along like a caterpillar heading for a particularly juicy leaf. Two shuffles then I stretch out my arm. The apples are still out of reach. I try again. I move forward, reach out and grab apple number one. *Got it! Now what do I do with it?* I look around and decide to tuck it into my T-shirt so I can hold on with both hands. The branch is definitely getting thinner.

My fingers reach all the way around the branch. *Have I grown a lot since I did this last year?* I stretch out to reach for another apple and hear a crack. I grab the second apple in one hand, hold on to the branch with the other, swing my legs down and jump to the ground before the branch with me on it breaks. I ignore the apples falling around my feet, reach into my T-shirt, pull out the first apple, and hold out a piece of fruit in each hand.

"Err! We're not eating those! Look at all the marks on them!" Raine shrieks.

"Cut!" I shout. "Did you get all of that, Ben?"

Ben nods and we all crowd around the iPad to watch the playback.

"Look! There's a soccer ball," Ben says, pointing to the screen. We all look from the iPad to the shed roof. "You could get a ladder and get that down if they asked you."

"Hmm, I like it," I reply, but feel unsure. I take a step back and look at the shed with my rectangle finger screen frame in front of my face. "I just have to find a way to make your orders look exciting for the viewer."

Everyone watches me as I rub my chin and imagine climbing up the ladder to get the ball. It's just too boring. But if the ball were further back on the roof, I would have to climb on top of the shed, and if I was on the roof I could...

"The High Fall Society!" I blurt out.

"What?" Ben asks.

"I have an idea," I say, running across the yard. "Help me with the trampoline."

The six of us stand around the circular trampoline and hold the metal frame. I can see the questions in everyone's eyes.

"We're going to put this under the gutter," I explain. "Then I'll climb up onto the roof, get the ball and fall off."

"Won't you get hurt?" Sunshine asks.

"No, my dad does it all the time, and besides we've been training for this haven't we?" I say, looking at Leila, Ben and Sam. "Now, on the count of three, one, two, three, lift!"

We half lift and half drag the trampoline into position and we all jump on. I can touch the gutter easily when I bounce, so it really isn't far to fall.

"We're ready for the shot. Clear the set. Raine, you can say..." I whisper some instructions and the twins sit back down at their table, giggling to each other.

Sunshine and Raine return to their nail polish, Ben gets the iPad ready and I walk back to the apples tree.

"Quiet on set...and action!" I say.

"Cinderella! There's a ball on the roof! I told you yesterday to put our things away. How dare you leave it outside?" Raine says confidently.

I hold out the two apples. Sunshine rolls her eyes at me and holds up the nail polish brush to explain her laziness. The look is perfect, even if it is the look Raquel gives me a hundred times a day.

I turn to the shed and quickly climb up, using the fence and window frame as foot holds then pulling myself onto the roof on my stomach. I hope Ben's catching all this on camera. I stand up and wonder whether the roof will take my weight. *Too late now.* Slowly and carefully I inch towards the ball. *Height is a really strange thing.* When I was jumping on the trampoline this roof didn't seem high, but now that I am on top looking down, my stomach feels all jittery.

"Hurry up, Cinder Slow Coach," Raine calls and then starts to giggle with Sunshine. "You still have to finish raking the leaves!"

Wow! They are really getting into this.

I lean forward and pick up the ball then wobble deliberately and jump. My arms wave in the air as I fall, the ball flies out of my hand, and just as I land on the trampoline, the ball crashes into the basket full of nail polish that is sitting on the table and sends bottles skywards. As they land, the glass bottles shatter, sending out a spray of purple, black, red and luminous orange polish all over Sunshine and Raine, who scream, jump to their feet and tip over the table.

Mom knocks on the kitchen window and we turn towards the noise. The twins look as if they have been to a

Splatter Paint Party. The table has multicoloured polish slowly dripping down the surface, like unstoppable rainbow lava, and the patio is covered with broken glass, an upturned basket and a collection of empty water glasses.

"That looked too dangerous, Maddie. Move that trampoline away from the shed and make sure you clean up after yourself," Mom says, as she disappears back inside. She reappears with a dustpan, brush, and newspaper to wrap the glass in, then turns and heads back into the kitchen.

"Is that it? Our mom would have killed us," Raine says, sounding astonished.

"This wouldn't happen at all at my place. I'm only allowed one friend at a time for play days unless it's my birthday," Leila comments, helping Sunshine to right the table.

I quickly sweep up the glass and wrap it carefully in the newspaper. Then take one of the extra sheets of paper and try to wipe up some of the spilt polish. Great smears of colour spread across our patio.

"The rain will wash the rest away," I say hastily, hoping I'm right, gathering all the garbage and placing it in the bin. "Come on, help me over here."

I run to the trampoline, closely followed by Ben and Sam. Leila, Sunshine and Raine look at the multicoloured polish drying on the table, shrug their shoulders and join us.

"Did you get all of that, Ben?" I ask as we move the trampoline back to its original position.

"I think so," he says.

"When do I get to do my part?" Sam asks.

"Soon," I say. "Very soon. Let's move on to the fairy godmother scenes. We'll collect the pumpkin, cats and hamsters..."

"Cats?" Ben questions.

"Hamsters?" Sam asks.

"We don't have any mice," I explain. "So we'll use my hamster, Snowy, and our class pet, Caramel, instead. The cats can turn into you two," I say, pointing to Ben and Sam. "We can use your cats, Cagney and Lacey, can't we?"

I don't wait for an answer. I just run over to our raised vegetable bed. There are three small, greenish pumpkins in amongst the runner beans and old lettuces. I pick up the largest pumpkin and start twisting it until it comes away with some leaves, vine and roots.

"Ben and Sam, run and get Cagney and Lacey. We'll get Caramel and Snowy. And we'll meet in front of the house," I say, then run up the back steps, two at a time. "Come on. We have a film to make."

A few minutes later, I'm sitting on the grass holding half an onion under my eyes until they sting and start to water. Sam is holding Cagney, Sunshine has Lacey and Raine is holding two quivering hamsters, one in each hand.

"Camera ready?" I ask. Ben nods. "Quiet on set! Rolling?"

"Err, I've pressed record," Ben replies uncertainly.

"Then we're rolling," I say, throwing the onion towards Ben's feet. "Action!"

Leila takes two steps forward and stands just behind my left shoulder. I look up with tears pouring from my stinging eyes.

"Who are you?" I ask, acting surprised.

"I am your fairy godmother and you will go to the ball," Leila says. "Fetch me a pumpkin."

I stand up, run out of shot, collect the pumpkin, run back into shot and place it on the ground.

"Now, get me two hamsters," Leila announces. The twins giggle quietly and Leila scrunches her face in an effort not to join in.

I know animals will do anything on camera for their favourite food. I have watched a monkey smile for a peanut, squirrels crawl over Veruca Salt for sunflower seeds and dogs lick their acting owners when chicken fat has been mixed into their make-up. I have even seen Mastiffs jump up and knock people to the ground when the stunt performers have liver pieces tucked under the collar of their costumes. So I have tucked some of Snowy's dried strawberry pieces between my fingers. I nod at Raine and she lowers the hamsters to the grass. Sam and Sunshine tighten their grip on the cats and I lower my hands to the ground. Raine lets go of the hamsters and slowly pulls her hands back onto her lap.

The hamsters stand in the grass looking around at their newfound freedom. We all hold our breath.

"Come on," I whisper.

Snowy is the first to move then Caramel follows. Slowly and cautiously they move towards my hands. It's working. Snowy takes a few steps forward then stops, her nose twitching in the air. Caramel copies. It's like playing Sneaky Statues.

"You can do it," I say.

I stay completely still. The shot is taking too long, but we can always cut out a section when we edit it. Two steps. Pause. They scurry forward. Pause. Snowy is almost at my hand. Should I lean forward and try to pick them up? I don't want to scare Caramel. So I wait and watch the twitching noses. I can feel Snowy's whiskers tickling my fingers.

Vrrrmmmm! Dad's motorbike starts, shattering the silence. Snowy sinks her teeth into my outstretched fingers. I jump up and scream in pain. Leila steps towards me and freezes in horror. Cagney's and Lacey's fur stands on end. Their bodies stiffen like soldiers standing to attention. They leap out of their keepers' arms and fix their eyes on Caramel. The chase is on.

Caramel turns and scampers across the grass, under the bench and around the rose bush.

"Get the cats!" I scream, with blood now dripping

down Snowy's coat, her teeth still embedded into the pad of my right index finger.

Sunshine runs around one side of the bench and Raine runs around the other. They both bend down to grab the cats at the same time. There's a loud crack as their heads meet in the middle, sending each of them flying backward onto the ground. Sam crawls under the bench and over the girls' legs. He throws his body forward attempting to catch Cagney but instead is snagged by his sleeve on the rose bush. Cagney turns on him, raises her back and hisses loudly. Meanwhile, Lacey is closing the gap between her and the hamster.

"There she is!" I shout, kicking out with my foot in an

attempt to show them the hamster running across the yard and into a bed filled with lavender, ferns and foxgloves. "Quick! The cats will kill her!"

Lacey utters a high-pitched meow, leaps over my extended leg and lands in a water-filled pot that is half covered with leaves. For a split second the furious cat stops dead, examines her soaking wet front legs then turns to the garage.

Caramel jumps out from under a fern and dashes for the cluttered workshop. Sunshine and Raine stagger toward the door trying to form a wall between our class pet and the cats. From either side of the yard, the cats charge at them and then jump.

"Help!" Sunshine and Raine scream, covering their faces.

The girls duck down and the cats fly over their heads.

"Watch out Dad!" I shout as the cats land and Cagney knocks over a large oilcan. Sam runs in after the cats, steps onto the growing pool of slick black liquid, slips over and lands on his back. A split second later he lets out a cry. Cagney and Lacey leap onto the pile of cardboard boxes, prowling angrily and trying to squeeze their fat bodies into any gaps they can fit a paw into.

"What the..." Dad says, turning off his motorbike and looking around at the chaos.

Two seconds later, the door from the mudroom swings open and Mom steps out to see a blood splattered hamster hanging from my outstretched hand; Sunshine and Raine crouched down on the driveway, holding their heads in their hands; Leila standing, looking very pale; Sam lying on his back covered in oil and Ben holding the iPad.

"Maddie! What is going on?" she shouts.

I look around slowly. *This was not the plan! And what is Ben doing?*

"Cut! Ben! Cut! This isn't part of the film!" I call out and slump down onto the grass. "Mom, it went wrong! All wrong!"

8

AN INVITATION FROM THE PALACE

"Maddie, we know where Caramel is hiding," Mom says calmly, putting a Band-Aid on my throbbing finger. "Give her time. She'll be terrified at the moment. Go and put some food there, it may tempt her out of hiding."

Just then the telephone rings and Mom goes to answer it.

"Don't worry, Maddie," Leila says, sliding a plate of cheese sandwiches towards me. "Caramel will be okay."

"What if she's not okay?" I panic. "What if she's died of fright? What if Cagney and Lacey had caught her? What will I tell Mr. Philips if we don't find her? What am I going to do?

"Food. We need food. Are there any strawberry treats left?" I ask, getting up from the kitchen table and taking a small plate from the cupboard. "Why did Dad have to start his motorbike right then? He hasn't used it for weeks."

"But it's cool," Ben says. "The tricks he does are awesome. I wish my dad could do the stuff he does."

"Yeah! Wheelies!" Sam shouts, jumping down from the table and running around the kitchen pretending to hold the handlebars of a motorbike.

"And stoppies!" Ben adds, making a screeching noise and throwing his weight forward as if he is balancing on the front wheel of a bike.

A smile twitches in the corner of my mouth. It is pretty cool when Dad does his tricks. No wonder they're used in so many movies... James Bond, *Charlie's Angels*, *Paddington*. We could use some motorbike stunts in *Cinderella*!

"That's it! I know who can be our messenger," I shout, racing towards the front door.

"Maddie," Mom calls. "That was Ivan's mom. He's finished playing hockey. He's just going to get into his costume so he'll be ready when he arrives."

"Sure, okay, whatever," I say whilst imagining the next shot. "Come on everyone. I have an idea!"

I run out the front door followed by the rest of the cast. The door bangs closed behind us. We charge down the steps and into the garage.

"Dad! Dad!" I shout. "Will you be the messenger from the palace? You could deliver the invitations for the ball on your motorbike and we could film you stunt riding all the way down the street."

Dad looks at our excited faces, smiles and says, "Sure."

"Yes!" I shout, punching the air. "I could be sweeping the path, then Dad, you could push me aside saying, 'Urgent message from the palace!' I'll fall into the leaves, but you'll ignore me and head straight for the door.

"Come on, we have work to do! Ben, grab the iPad. I'll get the broom and the rest of you cover this path with leaves."

We all run in different directions. By the time I get back, Sunshine, Raine, Leila and Sam are throwing huge handfuls of leaves all over each other and the path.

"Where did all these come from?" I ask.

Sam points down the street. There's a long trail of leaves that have been dropped on the ground. The trail leads all the way to Mrs. Green's front yard.

"Are you crazy?" I ask. "She'll eat you alive if she catches you."

Sam freezes for a moment then throws some leaves at me. The twins throw some at Sam, who bends down and collects more in his outstretched arms. The leaf fight is back on. Sam chases Sunshine, who quickly gathers a handful of damp leaves and tosses them over her shoulder. I toss mine towards Raine. There are leaves flying everywhere.

"Get her!" Raine laughs.

I catch some of the leaves and toss them straight back. Then pick up more and throw them as high as I can.

"Don't let them touch the ground!" I squeal, running

as fast as I can to catch the falling leaves until we hear the loud blast from an engine.

We look around to see Dad sitting on his motorbike wearing a black leather jacket and his helmet.

"Cool!" Ben shouts.

"Dad, ride to the corner. I'll drop my hand, like this, when I want you to start." I lift my hand above my head and drop it to my side. "Sunshine and Raine, you head inside and come out when you hear the bike. I'll be here sweeping. Does everyone know what they are doing?"

Dad nods his helmet up and down.

"Then places everyone! An Invitation from the Palace – take one," I announce.

Ben lifts the iPad and presses record as Dad revs his engine, pulls a wheelie and zooms off down the road.

I look around. The twins are standing outside the front door giggling and pointing to my dad. Ben has swung the camera around and seems to be filming them. *That could be a really good shot*, but there is no time to check right now.

"Ben, are you ready to roll?" I ask.

He presses the button to stop recording and gets ready to start again. I hold the broom in one hand and raise my other hand over my head. The twins squeal and head into the house. I can hear Dad's engine rev three times. My hand drops and I get to work.

Dad does a wheelie all the way up the road. It looks amazing! Then when he reaches our house he slams on the brakes and balances on the front wheel. When both wheels are on the road, Dad lowers the stand with his foot, switches off the engine and swings his leg over the seat.

Sunshine and Raine run down the steps arm in arm, giggling loudly. Dad strides along the path and pushes me aside, saying, "An invitation from the palace."

I do my best stunt fall onto the soft grass and the twins run up to my dad. He puts his hand into his jacket and pulls out an envelope. The girls grab it from him and run back into the house. Dad then jumps back on his bike, starts the engine and drives away.

"Cut! That was perfect!" I shout. "Let's take a look."

We all crowd around the small screen and replay the scene.

"Wow!" Sam says as he watches the bike in action.

"Oh, look at us!" Raine laughs.

"Nice fall," Ben says, smiling at me.

"Thanks," I say, turning red. "Good camera work."

Ben smiles and looks embarrassed. Then Sam jumps on him singing, 'We are the champions! We are the champions!' Ben pushes him off and Sam runs around the yard with his T-shirt pulled over his face as if he has just scored a goal in the Soccer World Cup.

Dad rides his bike onto the driveway and a car pulls up right behind him. Ivan's mother gets out and opens the back door. Ivan is slumped on the back seat with earphones firmly in place. He's wearing the costume he wore for the school play last year and a look that tells us his team didn't win the hockey tournament.

"It looks like Prince Charming has arrived," Dad says with his eyebrows raised. "So I'm going back to the garage."

"Let me know if you see Caramel," I shout after him.

"Ivan, you've got to see this," Ben says.

We all watch Ivan step out of the car in his snakeskin shoes; gold, skinny pants; red, orange and yellow, peacock feather shirt and jewel-covered crown. He takes out one white earpiece and watches the bike sequence in silence, shrugs his shoulders and turns to his mom with a pleading look.

"Goodbye, my darling," Ivan's mom says in a thick accent. "Call me, ven you are done."

"Mom," Ivan moans. "I don't want to be here."

They step aside and speak to each other in Russian. We all watch in silence until Mrs. Vladivenski pushes Ivan towards us, gets in the car and drives away. Ivan turns his back on us, sits under a tree, puts his earphone back in his ear and sulks.

We all look at each other. *Why is Ivan such a bad sport? None of us care about his stupid hockey game and whether he won or not! And what we can do with a miserable Prince Charming?* Then, I have an idea.

"Ivan, do you remember the Swan Lake show that came to school last year?" I ask.

"Yeah, it was lame," Ivan says without looking up from his phone screen.

"Yes," I agree, reluctantly. "But do you remember the prince? What was his name? Never mind. He was really miserable and didn't want to choose a wife. You can be just like that. Stay where you are and pretend you don't want to be here."

"That'll be easy enough," Ben says, rolling his eyes as I reach out and take the iPad and point the camera towards Ivan.

"Prince Charming, are you ready for the ball?" I ask in a deep voice.

"No, go away! Leave me alone!" Ivan replies.

"Your guests are arriving," I say, still pretending to be a palace servant.

"I don't care! I'm on level nine and I'm not doing anything until I'm on level fifteen!"

"Cut! Ivan, that was perfect!"

"Whatever," he whines without taking his eyes off the screen.

"Now," I say, turning to Sunshine and Raine. "We're going to get ready for the ball."

The twins run up the steps. I take Leila by the arm and follow them.

"What are you going to wear?" Leila asks.

"I don't know yet," I answer. "But I'll think of something."

From the top landing, I look down at Ben and Sam watching Ivan's game. Something in Ivan's face has softened. He's still concentrating on the screen but he seems to be happy now he's the centre of attention. *Making a film is very strange.* I turn, give Leila a hug and skip into the house.

9

AND THE CLOCK STRIKES TWELVE

A few minutes later, I emerge from the house in the purple sequined dress my mom wore to the World Stunt Awards. She hasn't worn it since, so I am sure she won't mind me borrowing it. The dress scrapes the ground despite the extra height Mom's high-heeled sandals give me.

"Careful," Leila says. "My mom says heels are bad for growing feet."

"I'm wearing them, not having them for dinner," I say.

It's hard to walk down the stairs. *How does anyone stay upright in these things?*

"No wonder Cinderella lost a shoe." I bend down, unbuckle the tiny clasp and hook the silver, sparkly straps over the fingers of one hand. "She must have been carrying them by the time she left the party.

"Ivan, let's film the prince and Cinderella while the twins are getting ready," I suggest. "When I agreed that they could be the Beautiful Sisters, instead of the Ugly Sisters, I had no idea it would take them this long to get into costume."

Ivan does not even look up from his game.

"He's on level twelve," Ben says, as if that explains why he is ignoring me.

"Well, I have an idea," I say. "You film me watching the prince playing his game and then we'll film him teaching me."

I tap Sam on the shoulder and toss my head, showing him it's time to get up. He sighs as he stands up and walks slowly over to Ben, who's ready to film. I hitch up the dress and take Sam's place, watching the game. *Ivan is really good at this.*

Partway through level thirteen, Sunshine and Raine come out of the front door in their matching white First Communion dresses. Ben turns the camera towards them and they flounce down the steps like movie stars, spinning around in unison when they reach the bottom.

"Wow!" Ben exclaims. "You look fantastic!"

The twins turn to each other, holding their clenched hands to their chins and giggling. Then Raine opens her arms wide, flutters her eyes at the camera and sweeps around in a circle to show off her dress. Sunshine copies. They are so excited that they jump up and down, trying different modeling poses and smiling huge metallic grins.

"Oi! You're meant to be filming me and the prince,

not the Ug... I mean Beautiful Sisters," I shout when I realize that Ivan has stopped playing.

Ben stops recording and turns back to the tree. A sigh and slow nod shows me he is ready to film us as directed, but his slumped shoulders and tight lips tell me a different story. I hold Ivan's phone in my hands and tap the screen to start the game.

Sunshine and Raine slump down, sit on the bottom step and rest their faces in the palms of their hands. Leila takes Sam by the hand and leads him into the garage. I can see them out of the corner of my eye, looking under Dad's tool cabinet in a desperate search for Caramel.

"We should do something with the others," I say.

"Just get to the next level," Ivan replies, grabbing his phone out of my hands and taking over the controls.

"No! Cut!" I announce, grabbing the phone back.

"Come on!" Ivan groans.

"We have quite enough of Cinderella and the prince. Let's move on to the scene where Cinderella leaves the ball," I say, jumping up and racing over to the steps. Sunshine and Raine move aside and look up into my eyes.

"Leila! Sam! We're going to need you," I call.

"I'll come out of the palace door," I say, pointing to our front door. "Then... that's it! I have a brilliant idea.

"I'll come out of here, followed by the prince. I'll trip and fall down the stairs with the shoes in my hands," I explain. "I'll drop one shoe, run across the grass and then jump into the carriage. Ben and Sam you'll pedal as fast as you can and we'll race down the road as the clock strikes twelve. Then we'll do a shot where I'm sitting on the ground and Leila, you can fly in."

"Fly?" Leila asks. "Maddie, I can't fly."

"Yeah, it's easy. Dad's flown me on the rigging at work, loads of times. I'll just get my climbing harness," I say. "Just wait here!"

I emerge from the house, with pillows tied to my front and back with belts around my chest, waist and hips, carrying my climbing backpack. I look enormous. Everyone looks up; they stare at me for a second, then burst into laughter.

"It's called padding," I say defensively. "A stunt performer has to use it to do a stair fall.

"Come on, Leila. I'll help you into my harness. We'll put it on back to front so the rope loop is at the back. Then you'll be able to fly like a real fairy."

"Maddie, I'm not sure..." Leila starts.

"Come on. This will be the best part of the film!"

I pull out a tangle of straps, show Leila where to place her legs and move the adjustable fasteners to her tiny body.

"I am going to feed this climbing rope down the back of your costume and attach it here," I say, lifting her dress and holding the strong material loop.

"Maddie! Everyone can see my underwear!" Leila whispers in horror.

"Then stop wriggling so I can tie a really good figure-of-eight knot," I say, mouthing the tying instructions to myself. "There. Now, take a few steps back and I'll throw the rope over that branch."

"Maddie! I'm not allowed to climb trees. Mom says they're dirty and dangerous!" Leila squeals.

"You're not climbing. You'll just be hanging under the branch as if you're covered in fairy dust. Then when you see the carriage, you'll be lowered to the ground so Cinderella can thank you for the wonderful night at the palace."

"I'm not sure..." Leila whines, looking worried and shaking her head.

"It's polite to say 'thank you' isn't it?" I question and Leila nods. "Then this *has* to part of the film."

I throw the loose end of the rope over a branch of the fir tree and pull Leila off the ground.

"Come on everyone," I call. "Give me a hand."

"Ouch! This hurts!" Leila calls as we pull on the rope.

"Don't worry," I say. "You won't be there long.

"Now, Sunshine and Raine, hold the rope and only lower Leila when I say so. Ready? Places everybody!"

Ben and Sam run to their bikes. Ivan and I run up the steps.

"Maddie!" Ben calls. "Who's going to film?"

I stop mid stride. There is a pause while I think.

"Ben, you can start the filming. Then, when I get to the bottom step, pass the iPad to Ivan," I say and the boys nod their heads, smiling at each other.

"We'll start when I say, 'Action!'" I explain, looking nervously at the stairs.

I've never done a stair fall before, but Dad says they are easy. "Just get as many pads on as you possibly can then tuck and roll, gravity does the rest," he always says.

"Tuck and roll. Tuck and roll," I whisper to myself.

When I reach the front door, I look out towards Sam sitting on his bike at the waiting carriage, Ben holding the iPad and Leila hanging in the tree.

"Rolling?" I ask Ben.

"Rolling," Ben replies and I push Ivan into the house. "Action!"

I swing open the door, making the boinging noise of a clock striking the hour, and run to the top of the stairs. Ivan is close behind me. I pretend to trip over and pause momentarily, crouching at the top of the wooden steps. It's a long way down.

Tuck and roll! Just go for it! I shout inside my head and tilt my body forward until I topple off my feet.

Ouch! I land heavily on my shoulder and scrape the back of my arm on the edge of a wooden step. *Ooo!* The back of my head bumps onto something hard as I roll over. *Oph!* My knees are pushed into my chest as I land on my shins, knocking out my breath. *Yow!* My shoulder is back on the stairs getting an extra bruise. *Ow, ow, ow, ow, OW!* I slide down the last few steps on my back and land on the concrete path on my bum. *Why didn't Dad ever tell me that this really hurts?!*

Jump up and run! I scream at myself, standing up painfully, limping for the carriage and carefully dropping a shoe on the way.

Ben throws the iPad up into the air and Ivan catches it neatly as I climb into the shopping cart. He jumps onto his bike and we take off down the road. *So far so good.* I turn around to see Ivan filming and Leila dangling from the fir tree behind him.

The shopping cart rattles as we gain speed. It feels as if my skeleton will fall apart. Blood is rushing around my body and I quickly look down to check it isn't gushing out of any of my injuries. Ivan runs along beside us with the iPad held out in front of him.

"We have to go around the block so we can get Leila in the shot," I shout towards Ivan.

"Car!" Ben hollers.

"Oh no! That's Leila's mom," I say turning back to see the danger ahead.

The two boys turn their bikes into the curb. The ropes between us loosen momentarily and then snap tight. The cart flies around the corner on two wheels.

"I don't have brakes!" I scream.

The carriage crashes into the bikes and stops abruptly. I, however, do not stop. I fly through the air, arms and legs waving against the nothingness of air.

"Tuck and roll, tuck and roll," I say, as I land with a thud in a huge pile of leaves.

I lay still for a second, checking that I haven't broken

any bones. *No, all in one piece.* The pillows have saved me. I raise my head, hoping for looks of amazement on the boys' faces. Instead I see terror.

"Get out of my yard, you hooligans!" Mrs. Green screams, running towards us with a rake in her hand. "It's taken me hours to fix the mess you made earlier."

I leap up, run back to our house and watch Mrs. Choudhury scrambling out of her car in a panic. Then she spots Leila hanging from the tree.

"Leila, what are you doing? Get down from there this instant!" she shouts, turning red in the face.

"I can't!" Leila cries.

"Let her down gently," I shout, but Sunshine and Raine lift their hands above their heads to show me that they are not holding the rope at all.

"Mommy, get me down!" Leila screams.

"It's okay, Leila. The rope's just got caught. I see the problem," I say, climbing the tree as quickly as I can.

"It is not okay!" Mrs. Choudury roars. "Leila is stuck in a tree and you think it is OKAY?!"

My eyes start to sting with the effort I am making not to cry. "She'll be down in a minute."

The rough bark scrapes my inner thigh as I crawl along the branch, grab hold of the rope in both hands and steady myself, ready to pull.

"Get ready to catch her!" I shout.

Sunshine, Raine, Ben and Sam all run under Leila's struggling feet and hold out their arms.

"No!" Leila yells as I pull the rope free with all my might.

Leila instantly plummets to the ground with the rope passing quickly through and burning my hands. I'm pulled sideways and only just manage to grab the branch, swinging one leg then the other towards the ground. Leila screams, Sunshine and Raine cry out, Mrs. Choudhury gasps and my dress tears, leaving a strip of sequins from the tree to my waist.

My ball gown has ripped but I don't care. My best friend just fell out of a tree and it's my fault, all my fault.

"Leila, are you okay?" I call, holding out my arms to help her up.

"Don't you touch my daughter!" Mrs. Choudhury screeches, taking Leila's hands and pulling her into a tight embrace. "What on earth do you think you were doing?"

"She was flying like a fairy," I explain.

"No, no, no! First her hair and now this! You are a liability, Madeleine Moore," Mrs. Choudhury shouts.

Leila looks down at the ground and starts to undo the harness. Her mother gathers the rope and throws it onto the back seat.

"Get in the car, Leila, we're going home."

"You can give the harness back to me on Monday. We'll finish the film another day," I say.

"No, no more! Leila will not be coming back. Ever! This is the last time you will put my daughter's life in danger!"

Leila looks terrified. She gets into the car and turns her face away from us. Everyone else looks at me. Mrs. Choudhury slams Leila's car door and opens her own. I take one look at her hard, cold face, burst into tears and run into the house.

10

THE PROBLEM WITH DOING NOTHING

"Maddie, I've made some hot chocolate," Mom whispers, placing her hand softly on the small of my back. "Sunshine and Raine just left. Ben and Sam have gone home. Ivan's the only one here and his mom'll come and pick him up when his brother's hockey tournament ends."

I raise my head off my tear-soaked pillow. My eyes sting and all I can think of is Leila being pushed into the car by her mother. Her words echo in my head: "Leila will not be coming back. Ever!"

"Did you call Mrs. Choudhury?" I sob.

"Not yet, but I will. Give her time to calm down a bit," Mom says.

"I wish I was dead," I cry.

Mom leans over, wipes a tear from my cheek with her thumb and kisses me gently on the forehead.

"Come through to the living room when you're ready. I'm sure Ivan would like some company."

Mom pulls a tissue out of the box by my bed and hands it to me.

I love my mom, but she just doesn't get it. *This is the worst day of my life.* I blow my wet, snotty nose. Why does your nose run when you cry? You don't suddenly catch a cold. *No! Don't get distracted! You are miserable, Maddie. A miserable failure!*

Slowly, I raise my body up off the bed and look down at myself. The pillows I attached to my front and back are still there. I look ridiculous. Slowly and cautiously, I touch the tender, puffy patch of purple skin on my shoulder. *Ouch!* I feel the bump on the back of my head. *Ow!* And breathe in quickly through gritted teeth as I touch the grazes down my shins. *So much for padding!*

I swing my legs over the side of the bed and look down at the huge graze on my inner thigh. That must have happened when I dropped from the tree. I couldn't feel it before, but now that I have seen it through the huge rip in the dress, it stings like crazy.

I tear the pillows off and throw them onto the floor. The dress, however, is harder to remove. The tape Leila used to make the dress fit, is stuck to the sequins and my shoulder aches every time I reach behind my back. *I've ruined Mom's new dress*, I think, letting it fall to the floor.

Finally, I stand in my underwear and look in the mirror. I pull two leaves out of my tangled hair. My eyes are red, my skin is blotchy and my body aches from the inside out. *I wish I could just hide in my room. If only Fred and George Weasley's Skiving Snackboxes were real. I would eat one and barf every morning for the rest of my life and never come out of my room again. Then I'd eat the antidote, have hot chocolate and cookies and watch movies for...ever!*

I sigh and slowly pull on some leggings and a T-shirt, open my door and limp down the hallway. I wish Ivan had gone home like the others. I really don't want to see anybody.

As I walk into the living room, I see my dad sitting on

the sofa. He holds out his arms. I run to him and bury my head in his shoulder. I can feel his big strong arms around me.

Mom brings in a tray with four mugs of hot chocolate and a plate of home-baked cookies. She turns to Ivan. *She is so English. Even in the middle of this complete disaster she sticks with 'guests come first.'*

When I look up to take a steaming mug of hot chocolate in one hand and a cookie in the other, I can see that Ivan has his head down, looking at a game on his phone. *Does he get a pain in his neck from sitting in the same position for so many hours each day?* I move to copy the way he is sitting, then shift again because my neck aches.

Mom takes the Marx Brothers DVD collection off the bookshelf, opens it and fiddles with three remotes until the familiar, grainy, black-and-white titles appear on the screen. No one speaks.

I smile to myself when I see the four live ducks swimming in a cauldron with a fire underneath it. *Did they ever have to think about animal welfare in the 'Olden Days?'* Then I remember Caramel. *OMG! I hope I can find her before Monday. I can't go to school without her.* My stomach lurches and I look up.

Ivan has stopped playing the game on his phone and is watching the TV. His blond eyebrows have almost formed one line. He looks as if he's watching something in a foreign language.

A newspaper headline appears on the screen announcing "Firefly: The New Leader of Freedonia."

"What is this?" Ivan asks scornfully.

"The Marx Brothers," I say in astonishment. *How could anyone live for ten years without knowing Groucho, Harpo, Chico and Zeppo?*

"The who?" Ivan asks.

"That's Groucho with the big, black mustache and cigar," I say, pointing to the screen and laughing as the actor wakes to the sound of an alarm clock, tears off his nightshirt and cap to reveal a suit underneath. He then leaps off his bed, slides down a firefighter pole and arrives at the back of the formal reception.

"Are we waiting for someone?" Groucho, Dad and I say together.

Everyone on the screen turns to look at Groucho and sings operatically, "Firefly! The Leader of Freedonia!"

"They sound weird," Ivan says.

"Yeah," I admit. "But just wait until Groucho dances."

"My phone battery is nearly dead," Ivan grumbles.

Argh! This is not about you, Ivan! Just let me enjoy my movie.

"Do you have a charger for this? My dad got it for me when I won the science competition, but it's so new that no one has the right charger for it," Ivan complains.

Dad squeezes my shoulder and Mom rests a hand on my leg. I know they want to make everything okay again, but it won't be. Ivan's life is going on just as it was before.

But mine has stopped. Nothing will ever be the same again. Did the Marx Brothers ever have a mother take them away from the film set? Did they ever have a neighbour chase them with a rake? Did they ever lose the class pet or get someone stuck in a tree?

My eyes start stinging and I feel as if I am going to start crying again. I look down and pull my knees up to my chest. I can't even hug the warm mug because of the rope burns on my palms. I glance at the DVD box lying on the coffee table. Mom has glued a bright yellow postcard to the outside of the box. There's a picture of Groucho Marx smiling up at me with a cigar in his hand and a sparkle in his eyes. There's a speech bubble that reads, "The problem with doing nothing is that you never know when you are finished."

I find myself arguing with an imaginary Groucho Marx in my head:

Me: *It's okay for you. You had your brothers. I have no one.*

Groucho: *We had sets that wobbled, black-and-white film, bad jokes and we still made people laugh.*

Me: *We didn't even finish filming.*

Groucho: *And you won't finish while you're sitting watching me. Just look at you. 'I never forget a face, but in your case I'll make an exception.'*

I lift up my head in time to see Groucho and Harpo's slapstick mirror routine.

"You have to watch this," I say to Ivan, who's looking out the window.

He turns back to the TV and watches Harpo copying Groucho's moves.

"We did this in Drama when that actor came into school," Ivan says dismissively.

"Yes, but look at all the things they do," I laugh as Groucho moves his glasses, crawls on the floor and picks up a hat in an attempt to show up Harpo.

"You were funnier in class and had way better ideas filming today," Ivan insists.

"Better than the Marx Brothers?!" I say.

"Well, I wasn't there for all the filming, but what I saw looked pretty good. Look. They're just chasing each other like they're playing tag. Your carriage was brilliant," Ivan says.

I look at Ivan. People never stop surprising me. *That comment wasn't even about him.*

"I don't know what Ben managed to get, but when I was filming, it looked awesome," Ivan finishes and turns back to the window to see if there is any sign of his mom.

I sit for a moment thinking about all the scenes we shot that day, the apples, the invitation from the palace, rescuing the soccer ball... There were some pretty good moments. I smile to myself and wonder whether we have enough to make the film.

"Mom, can we use your computer?" I ask.

"Sure," Mom says, looking confused.

"Ivan, let's download today's shots and see what we've got."

Ivan looks up at me with questioning eyes. Mom smiles and shakes her head. Did I see her roll her eyes in Dad's direction?

"That's the spirit, Princess," Dad says, winking at me.

I jump to my feet. "Come on. We have a film to make and I have an idea about how we're going to do it!"

11

KARMA FOR THE CARAMEL KILLER

"Come on Maddie, breakfast," Mom calls for the third time.

"Mom, I can't go to school today..." I moan from under my duvet.

"You can and you will," Mom replies in a tone that means she's not in a mood to be messed with.

"I'll come in with you and we'll speak to Mr. Phillips together," she adds, her tone softening a little. "You won't be the first or the last child to lose a class pet over a weekend."

"It's not just that," I continue, but when I look up from under my bedding Mom has already left my room. *Why don't grown-ups get it? My BFF's mother hates me and hasn't allowed me to speak to, or text, Leila since she left my place. The class geek wants me to spend every waking hour in front of a computer screen editing a film that we'll probably never finish. There's still no sign of Caramel even though I've tried every piece of advice I could find on YouTube. Raquel is bound to find out that her fan club spent Saturday working with 'The Enemy.'*

And...OMG! I have nothing to wear. I want to blend in today. I want to be the same as everyone else. I want to be invisible. I can't wear anything too bright. I can't wear anything with a logo from a film or TV series. I don't want to wear anything that will rub on my cuts and scrapes, but I have to find something that will cover the bruises.

I take out items of clothing one at a time and toss them onto the armchair in the corner of my room. *If only I could stay here and curl up on that chair all day.*

"Maddie, where are you?" Mom calls from the kitchen.

"Coming," I reply as I pull on some pants, a T-shirt and a sweatshirt.

"I just want to check the garage one more time to see if there's any sign of Caramel," I explain as I walk into the kitchen.

"Take something with you or you'll run out of time to eat."

Mom thrusts some food in my direction. I press two pieces of toast together to make a peanut butter, honey and banana sandwich and start to remove the rolled up towels I put down to block the gap at the bottom of the door.

Slowly, I open the garage door with my free, slightly sticky hand. It's dark inside. I flick the light switch and the fluorescent tube flashes into action. Eating my breakfast sandwich, I move towards the hamster cage. Caramel is not asleep in her bed. I check the six food dishes placed carefully around the garage. There are three pieces of dried sweet corn, two sunflower seeds and a slice of dried strawberry in each dish, just as I left them. Caramel has not eaten her favourite snacks. I examine the flour sprin-

kled on the floor. There are no paw prints. *Nothing!*
Nada! Zilch!

"Any sign of her?" Dad asks from the doorway.

I shake my head, tear off a bit of my sandwich and place it into Caramel's cage.

"Well, I'd run home for that!" Dad says, looking hungry.

I hold out my food and he takes an enormous bite.

"I wish you could take me to school today," I say, looking up at him with big puppy dog eyes.

"Sorry love, I would if I could but I have an audition this morning," Dad says softly.

"Oh yeah. I forgot." I sigh, feeling really bad. "Good luck!"

"You too, Princess. Although I know you... When the going gets tough," Dad sings with a cheesy grin on his face and a pretend microphone in his hand.

"The tough get going," we sing together, touching the knuckles of our closed right fists and letting our hands explode away from each other.

Twenty minutes later, Mom and I are emerging from my classroom and I walk her towards the school door. I can't believe what just happened. Mr. Phillips only took the briefest of pauses from writing on the whiteboard when Mom told him about losing Caramel.

"Oh well, she'll probably turn up when she's hungry," he said, glancing at the clock. "Perhaps you could tell everyone about your YouTube research and all the things you're doing to get her back. Now, I have to finish getting ready for our day. If there's nothing else, I'll see you in a few minutes."

Nothing else? Come on! Get real! This is a disaster! Caramel's probably been eaten by an owl or mauled by a cat by now. This is going to be a 'News Flash' story. Everyone is going to remember me as Caramel's murderer. I won't be able to show my face and my teacher is worried about whether Language Arts comes before Math or after Library.

"Now, that wasn't so bad, was it?" Mom asks as she pushes open the front door. "Everyone will understand."

"Sure," I say sarcastically, looking out into the grey October morning and spotting Raquel jumping rope with Sunshine and Raine. "My day is getting better by the minute."

"Five, six, seven, eight," Raquel squeals with laughter as she counts and the twins turn the long piece of rope between them.

"Go and play with your friends," Mom says, giving me a kiss then striding towards the gate.

What friends? I look around the playground. Leila is nowhere in sight. I can't see Ben. Ivan has hockey practice on Mondays, Wednesdays and Fridays, so I can't even talk to him about the film. I'm on my own.

I walk back towards the school building, willing the bell to ring. Instead, I tune in to the words Raquel is chanting. "Cinderella, dressed in yella, went upstairs to meet a fella. On the way she ripped her dress. How many hamsters died in the mess? One, two, three, four..."

Sunshine suddenly stops turning the rope when she sees me. Raquel and Raine both turn to see why their fun is being interrupted.

"I heard about your attempt to make a film," Raquel sneers, linking arms with Sunshine and Raine. "Come on, her failure is just karma for trying to steal friends for her pathetic ideas! Karma for the Caramel Killer!"

The first bell rings. *Why are there times when it feels as if I have shoes made of concrete?* I know I have no choice. I have to go into school, climb the stairs, get my planner out of my bag and go to my desk. But today my head is pushing my body against its will. *How many more years do I have to do this for, anyway? Grade five, grade six, grade seven...*I count on in my head, taking a heavy step with each number. *Eight more years!*

Finally, I reach the classroom and look at the tangle of bags, bodies and coats in the cloakroom area. There are just too many people in too small a space. I honestly think I could barf.

Leila's not at her coat hook. *Where is she?* My brain starts whirring. *Maybe her mom has locked her in a tower or maybe the fall hurt her back and she'll be in a wheelchair the rest of her life or maybe...*

"Hey, Maddie!" Ivan calls from the hallway. Some of his hair is stuck to his forehead with sweat. *Boys are so gross.* "I've put all the shots in order and have a list of the scenes we're missing."

He grabs a wad of papers from his bag and thrusts them into my hand as the second bell rings. It's a couple of seconds before I realize he's talking about *Cinderella.*

"Some we can animate. Some we can fill in with pretend newspaper headlines but some we're going to have to film. There's an editing timetable here," he says, taking the papers back and turning to the last page.

"Mr. Vladivenski and Miss Moore, are you going to join us today?" Mr. Phillips asks as the introduction to 'O, Canada' plays over the PA and everyone looks at us as they scrape their chairs over the floor to stand behind their desks.

When we've heard the English and French versions of the national anthem, we all sit down and Mr. Richardson's voice crackles through the speaker above the white board. "This week we are all going to think about focus. An ability to focus is essential in a good learning environment..."

I take out my planner and start to stuff Ivan's notes into my desk. Mr. Phillips is marking our math tests so I start to flick through the pages in front of me. Ivan has the whole film mapped out: the newspaper headline announcing the prince's ball, Cinderella being bossed around by the Ugly Sisters, the arrival of the fairy godmother, the ball, the journey home, the shoe fitting and the marriage. *OMG! This must have taken hours. He really thinks this is possible.*

I feel bad that I haven't really thought about the film since I gave him a USB stick with Saturday's downloads. But, then again, I was trying to find a hamster, invent excuses to text Leila from Mom's phone and figure out how I was going to survive school without a BF.

Ivan passes me a note. I open it and read, "I have highlighted the scenes we did on Saturday." I look over my shoulder and mouth, "Obviously." Then, feeling bad, I turn around again and whisper, "Thanks. This looks good."

"Maddie and Ivan, listening please," Mr. Phillips reminds us and I turn around.

"When something distracts you, record it," Mr. Richardson continues. "Then figure out how to put it aside so you can focus!"

I turn to the editing schedule. Ivan has listed every Saturday and Sunday between now and the competition deadline. But next to every date he has written, "Only possible if we get kicked out of the hockey tournament but we won't. We're the best!" Then he has listed the Computer Club lunchtime sessions. *I hate being inside at lunch times.*

"Maybe I should take that," Mr. Phillips says, making me jump. He holds out his hand and takes Ivan's notes. Raquel, Sunshine and Raine all giggle, but when I look at them the twins stop and look at the floor. Raquel glares at them.

"Some of you may struggle to focus on your work this week, but even with our Halloween Dance on Friday..." A chorus of cheers, followed by chatter about costumes, drowns Mr. Richardson's voice out.

"Quiet!" Mr. Phillips calls over the noise.

"Don't lose valuable learning time. Now, on Friday, you may bring a costume to change into at lunchtime but please be mindful that we have some children who find Halloween frightening. No one will be allowed to wear a mask or any gory make-up.

"Let's all have a week full of focused attention to our work and a fun, safe celebration on Friday. Happy learning!" Mr. Richardson concludes to a universal chorus of groans.

"I haven't quite finished marking your math tests just yet. But from those I've looked at, you could do with some more practice," Mr. Phillips says, handing out a sheet with twenty-five long multiplication questions on it.

Reluctantly, I pick up my pencil and start working. I'm only on question three and feeling very bored. *Where is Leila? She's never late.* Then I wonder whether Leila or my work is the distraction I should record and figure out how to put aside. My train of thought is broken when the door opens and Leila walks in and takes off her coat, hat, scarf and gloves even though it's not that cold out. *What will she wear when it snows?* She takes her planner out of her bag, picks up a chair from the back of the room and sits at her desk.

"Morning, Leila. Glad you could join us," Mr. Phillips says, handing her a worksheet.

"Where were you?" I whisper.

"Mom was signing me up for lunchtime yoga, and asking about the Computer and Science Clubs. She wants me to do supervised activities or go home for lunch," Leila admits.

"What?!" I mouth.

Leila shrugs, looks at her math, picks up a pencil and starts working.

This is outrageous! First Leila's not allowed to come to my place. Now we can't have lunchtimes together. This will kill me. No! Wait! I have an idea. I tear a corner out of the back of my planner and write "I'll see you in Computer Club. Show this to Ivan."

I carefully fold the note and write "Leila. BFF" on the outside then slide it onto her desk. She opens it, reads it, smiles in my direction, folds it again, crosses out her name and writes "Ivan" on the front then puts it on his desk. Ivan opens the note, reads it, smiles at me and puts it in his pocket.

I am totally focused for the rest of the morning, figuring how we can film every incomplete scene.

When the bell rings for lunch, Mr. Phillips stands up and gives me back Ivan's plans for *Cinderella*.

"I don't want to see these in class again," he says. "But they look interesting. Good luck."

"Thanks," I say, feeling embarrassed and quickly getting up to get my lunch.

"Eat up fast," I say to Leila and Ivan. "We have work to do."

12

COMPUTER CLUB

Mr. Richardson looks up from his work and raises his eyebrows at me as we enter the computer room.

"This is a club for students who want to quietly improve their computer skills," Mr. Richardson explains.

I nod, grab a chair and sit down at Ivan's side. Gradually, other children enter and switch on computers around the room. There's a group of Korean boys who all enter passwords and start playing Spycraft. There's the weird grade seven boy, William, wearing a top hat and tails. He edits the school newspaper and says he was named after the royal prince. Then there's George, the Greek Geek from our class, who is always talking about tanks, Star Wars and Lego. *Wow, what a bunch of weirdoes!*

"Look at this!" Ivan whispers excitedly. "I thought this could come before the announcement of the ball."

Ivan presses play and six animated musicians lift

trumpets to their mouths and play an arrival call. I'm impressed.

"Then I have this," Ivan adds, tapping and clicking frantically until an image of a newspaper front page spins on the screen, comes to a stop and zooms in to reveal the headline, "Prince Comes of Age: Palace to Host Party to Celebrate."

"Ivan, they're brilliant!" I whisper.

I pick up Ivan's notes and flick through the pages. There are a lot of scenes that haven't been highlighted.

"These can all be done using Khan Academy software." Ivan points to the scenes that have KA written after them. "And these scenes are mostly about me. We could film these at your place if we ever loose a hockey game."

"Sorry," I say to Leila, who shrugs her shoulders but looks as if she may cry.

"But what about the ball?" I ask, hoping to change the subject.

"The fairy godmother wasn't at the ball," Leila mumbles. "You don't need me at all."

"Yes we do!" I say. "You're the perfect person to get away with being a camera operator."

"When? How? Maddie, what are you talking about?" Leila asks.

"The Halloween Dance. I'll patch up Mom's dress and pretend I go to *Monster High*. Ivan, you can come as a ghost of a Russian prince and tie your cape around your head so it looks as if you've been beheaded. The twins can come in their First Communion dresses and be the brides of Dracula. It'll be perfect!"

"Except for one small thing," Leila says. "We're not allowed to take photos at the dance."

"Unless..." I look from Leila to William then back to her. "You're the reporter for the school newspaper. If William, as the editor, gets you to do a story on the dance, we could film as much of the dance as we want to. Go on! Go and ask him!"

I push Leila out of her seat. Ivan and I peek around the computer as a red-faced Leila walks across the room. She looks back at us and I smile encouragingly. *Come on. You can do it! You can speak to a boy you don't know.*

I can see her lips moving and the newspaper guy looks up from his screen.

"Is everything okay?" Mr. Richardson asks.

"Yeah. Just sorting out who's going to write a report on the Halloween Dance," the editor explains, looking pleased.

"Yes! Cinderella will go to the ball." I cheer under my breath.

I put out my hand, Ivan places his on top of mine, and then Leila puts her hand on the top.

"One for all," I mouth.

"And all for one!" Ivan and Leila join in with me.

We raise our hands into the air and turn our attention to our unfinished competition entry.

13

MADELEINE MOORE TO THE OFFICE

"Snow!" I yell, running into the playground and trying to catch the huge flakes on my tongue.

Leila is behind me, struggling with her hat, scarf and gloves. I pick up a handful of snow and throw it at my BF.

"No snowballs allowed!" Ivan shouts, running past me, throwing an enormous snowball in my face and skidding down the hill.

"That's it!" I screech, picking up snow from the ground and running after him.

"Madeleine Moore! You know the rules! No snow-balls allowed!" Mme Perdu's shrill voice calls.

"But..." I say.

"No buts."

I drop my snowball and watch our duty aid walk away. THWACK! Ivan's snowball gets me right in my back.

"Ignore him, Maddie. If you get called to Mr. Richardson's office again, you'll be moved to another class and I'll have to stay inside doing supervised activities for the rest of my life," Leila pleads. "Look, there's Ben."

I turn and see him on the wobbly walkway over the monkey bars.

"Come on. I have an idea," I say, climbing onto the equipment.

"Ben, let's be polar explorers," I shout, running and jumping until the blue chains and plastic planks shake. We jump from the bridge to the platform near the fire-fighters pole, kicking the snow from under our feet.

"If your feet touch the ground, you'll sink into the frozen sea," I explain, holding the railings and shaking the equipment.

"Hey," Raquel whines, stepping out from the semi-shelter of the climbing wall tower with the twins close behind her. "Some of us need to stay dry."

"Man overboard!" I shout, lying on my stomach, holding out my hand to Sunshine and ignoring Raquel.

Sunshine looks up at us with panic in her eyes and a hairbrush in her hand.

"Come on! You'll drown in the icy waters," I explain, trying to get Sunshine to join in our game.

"Some of us have better things to do than play your silly games," Raquel says, looking at me as if I was dog poop on her shoe. "I *have* to stay clean and dry today for my new publicity photos this afternoon.

"When we win the Young Filmmakers Award, I am getting a proper agent. Oh, have you heard? My drama school has been nominated for Best Film. We got our tickets on Saturday. Of course we'll win. We always do. Oh, whatever happened to your pathetic attempt."

I look blank. It'd been weeks since I sent off *Cinderella* and I'd not heard a thing. Raquel had a nomination and I didn't. *All that work for nothing!*

"You can brush my hair over there." Raquel grins, linking arms with Sunshine and Raine. "What do you think I should wear to the awards? Of course, you two can come as my guests. Maybe next year your names will be at the top of the waiting list and you'll be part of the winning team."

With that, Raquel looks up at me, throws her hair over her shoulder and, leaves me lying on my stomach. Snowflakes land gently on my head. My long, curly hair is a freezing bird's nest. My snowsuit feels damp and my fingers tingle in the cold. I can see my breath, but it feels as if all the life has been knocked out of me.

Leila and Ben come and sit beside me.

"Don't let her get to you," Leila says.

"Maybe your invitation just hasn't arrived yet," Ben tries.

I sit up slowly, pull my knees into my chest and look across the playground. Raquel has gone and my friends are right here, with me.

"Come on," I say, jumping to my feet. "We're trapped in the polar ice. The boat is going to get crushed."

Ben and Leila look a little confused then realize we're playing our game again. "Abandon ship!"

We run onto the high walkway and Ben reaches for the firefighter pole.

"Your feet can't touch the ice," I remind Ben, and he swings his body around the pole, back onto the platform.

"Follow me," I call, climbing over the dirty red rope bridge onto the tall pyramid. "We can look for land from the top."

"Can we play?"

I look down. Sam and Zack are standing on the wood chips underneath us.

"Sure. You can be penguins," I say "We're explorers, stuck in ice. We're going to catch you for our dinner."

Sam and his BF scream and run around the equipment. I jump from one piece of rope to the next, trying to catch them. Ben copies me and Leila edges along, holding on tightly to the upright ropes.

Ivan skids across the wood chips, catches Sam and brings him to me.

"Yes, you look good for dinner," I say.

I grab Sam's hands and Ivan tries to lift the wriggling penguin onto the equipment. Zack runs to help his friend, grabs Ivan's pants and tries to pull him away. Ben moves around the spider's web until he is next to me and able to put one arm around my waist.

"Pull!" I shout. "We need food or we'll starve."

Our game is interrupted by the sound of the buzzer. Our bodies slump. *This should be a snow day. We're having way too much fun to go inside.*

"Madeleine Moore and Ivan Vladivenski to the office, please" Mrs. McIntyre announces over the PA. "That's Madeleine Moore and Ivan Vladivenski to the office."

"What?!" I panic, letting go of Sam's hands.

I look around. Mr. Richardson is standing on the steps leading to the gym. Ivan, Ben and Leila follow my gaze. Our principal turns and walks inside. *How much of our game did he see?*

I stand frozen to the spot, searching my brain for any other reason for this call to the office. My mind is blank and my heart is racing. I can hear Raquel's laugh. I screw up my face and glare at her.

"Go on," Leila says, looking worried.

Here I go again! I say to myself, climbing down from

the spider's web and glancing at Ivan. We start walking. *At least we're in this together.* Everyone seems to look at us as they hurry to their classrooms. *I hate this walk, over the wood chips, across the basketball court, towards the school doors and into the dragon's lair.*

The heat of the office hits me as soon as I open the door. Ivan stamps his feet on the mat, wipes snow off his jacket, shakes his head like a wet dog and then starts styling his hair with his fingers. Mrs. McIntyre looks up from her computer when droplets of water land on her work. She stares at us over the rims of her glasses, shakes her head and grins.

"You can knock on Mr. Richardson's door. He's expecting you," she says.

Melting snow drips down my neck and I have a sick feeling in my stomach. Ivan steps forward and knocks on the door.

"Come in," Mr. Richardson's voice booms from inside.

Ivan and I look at each other. I reach out, turn the door handle and let Ivan step in first.

"Well, it looks as if you've had fun in the snow," Mr. Richardson starts.

"It was Maddie's idea," Ivan interrupts. "I only joined in right at the end."

So much for being in this together.

"Well, I'm pleased some of Maddie's ideas have excellent outcomes," Mr. Richardson continues.

Ivan and I look at each other. I am totally confused.

What is Mr. Richardson talking about? Best not to say anything right now.

"I have just read an email from The Young Filmmaker of the Year Awards," Mr. Richardson says. "You have both received a nomination for an award. Congratulations!"

Ivan and I look at each other again. It takes a second for the news to sink in, but when it does relief and joy burst out together.

"We did it!" I shout, jumping up and down.

"We've won!" Ivan yells.

"A nomination does not mean you've won," Mr. Richardson explains. "But it does mean that your entry has been singled out as one of the best."

I can hardly believe what I'm hearing. My open fingers are clutching my cheeks, my mouth is open and my eyes are popping out of my head. It's as if a full Santa sack has suddenly appeared in front of me. The only sound I am able to make is a tiny squeak.

"Perhaps you could lead an assembly about making the film," Mr. Richardson suggests, and I nod, not really listening.

"Your tickets for the awards will be sent to school, and I will make sure Mr. Phillips gets them to you. I will pass this excellent news on to your parents straight away, but I am sure you would like to be the ones to let your friends know. So, I'll let you get back to class."

"Thank you," Ivan and I say together, turning around and racing for the door.

Once we leave the office, Ivan and I leap about screaming. I don't care who we disturb. We did it! This is the best school day, ever!

"Come on!" I yell. "We've got to tell Leila. I can't wait to see the look on Raquel's face when she hears. We might win."

"What do you mean, 'might,'" Ivan shouts, leaping up and punching the air. "I am the greatest. Of course, I'll win."

"We'll see about that," I say. "Race you back to class."

14

AND THE WINNER IS...

"Do you think they'll come?" I ask Mom.

I look around at the growing crowd gathering in the foyer of the theatre attached to our local high school.

"Mrs. Choudhury accepted the invitation so I know they'll be here," Mom says calmly as the theatre doors open.

I wish I had my mom's confidence. My stomach is full of butterflies and the palms of my hands feel sweaty. I can hardly believe that *Cinderella* got finished, let alone received two nominations for awards. I wave to Ivan across a sea of pink Dominic Drummond Drama, 3D Acting for Life T-shirts. How did Raquel's theatre school get so many tickets? I was only given six. They seem to have sixty and, of course, there she is in the centre of it all, lapping up the attention from her acting school buddies and ignoring Sunshine and Raine. Her mother is talking to the guy who came into our school and gave us acting classes in grade four. He's looking around and moving his flock towards the open doors. Raine looks over in my direction and mouths, "Good luck."

"Maddie!" Leila shouts, running towards me and giving me a hug.

"Congratulations on your nomination, Madeleine, it seems as if you have some talent for making films," Mrs. Choudhury says, smiling and moving her head in a way that is not quite a nod and not quite a shake.

She spoke. She actually spoke to me. This is the first time Leila's mom has spoken to me since the tree incident. I don't know whether to laugh or cry. I grab Leila's arm and whisper in her ear, "Does this mean we can spend time together again?"

Leila shrugs her shoulders and smiles at me as we move towards the theatre doors. I am arm in arm with my BFF. My whole body is buzzing with excitement. This is turning into the best day of my life.

Inside the theatre, there's a hustle and bustle as people find their seats, remove their coats and settle down. On stage there's a microphone, a table full of golden cups and a huge cinema screen that reads "Welcome to the Tenth Young Filmmaker of the Year Awards".

OMG! I am actually here. Sitting at the award ceremony. There are so many cups. Maybe I could win an award. I could actually beat Raquel. I imagine walking onto the stage and collecting a prize.

"Do you have your winner's speech ready, Maddie?"

Mr. Phillips says, shaking hands with Mom, Dad and Mrs. Choudhury.

Mr. Phillips! What's he doing here?

"Thank you for the invitation." Mr. Richardson's voice makes me turn around quickly.

My principal is moving into a seat that's almost behind mine. He is wearing jeans with heavily stitched patches showing some fraying denim, an open-neck white shirt and an expensive-looking jacket. He smiles at me and I feel blood rushing to my face. He does look like a model when he smiles.

"Glad you could make it," Mr. Vladivenski says, shaking Mr. Richardson's hand. "Just look at what these children are capable of when they have the right equipment. Imagine what they could do if every child had their own tablet. The boys would be excited about coming to school and..."

Mr. Vladivenski goes on and on about getting more high-tech stuff for the school. Surely Ivan didn't invite teachers as his guests. But how else would they have gotten the tickets?

"What the heck!" I mouth at Ivan, who smiles at me and shrugs his shoulders as the lights dim.

A man wearing a black suit and black bow tie walks onto the stage. He is arm in arm with the most beautiful girl I have ever seen.

"It's Rockin' Robyn!" I whisper to Leila.

"Who?" Leila replies.

"Rockin' Robyn. From Robyn Records," I say urgently with my mouth hanging open. "You know, the TV show."

"Oh, yeah," Leila says, realizing that the person on stage is the same person whose picture is on the poster on my bedroom wall.

She's wearing huge heels and a hot pink dress that's so tight it looks as if she can't breathe let alone walk across the stage. Wow! This is amazing. It's just like the Oscars.

The walk to the microphone takes an age. *Robyn looks weird, amazing but weird. Doesn't she wear Rock Chick clothes all the time?* I take off my black felt trilby hat and place it on the floor under my seat. My eyes drift across the audience. One family is switching places with each other so the smallest can see. Most of the adults are glancing down at their programs or whispering to each other. Children are wriggling in their seats in an attempt to get a better view.

"It's Rockin' Robin" can be heard as a buzz passing through the audience. "You know, Robyn Records."

Everyone's excited. Everyone except Raquel. Her body's slumped down, one elbow resting on the arm of the chair with her head in her hand. *I can't believe this bores her.*

"Ladies and gentlemen, boys and girls." The man's deep, booming voice fills the room. "Welcome to the Tenth Young Filmmaker of the Year Awards. We had a record number of entries this year and the standard of filmmaking gets better and better. You are all champions.

Everyone who entered deserves a prize. To finish a film requires dedication, imagination, teamwork and incredible determination."

"Sure does," Ivan whispers, tapping me on the shoulder.

"But enough from me. You're all here to find out if you have won an amazing prize from one of our sponsors," Mr. Booming Voice announces, stepping away from the microphone.

Company logos flash up on the screen and Robyn smiles in my direction. My stomach tightens and I grab Leila's arm. *This is it!*

"Best Costume this year is awarded to..." Mr. Booming Voice fumbles with an envelope and pulls out a card with a gold cup printed on the back. "Dominic Drummond Drama for the film *The Seven Dwarves Meet Snow White.*"

The sea of pink erupts with shouts of hooray, clapping and cheering. The acting teacher grabs the child sitting beside him by the hand and moves along the line of students as quickly as his oversized belly allows. He looks surprised, but I can tell it's fake by the way he keeps thanking everyone who makes room for him and pats him on the back. Finally, they make it onto the stage. Dominic shakes hands with Mr. Booming Voice, gives Robyn a kiss on each cheek, takes the cup, holds it high, then hands the cup to the student standing red-faced beside him and looks up at the screen.

There's a slide show of the costumes, the queen, dwarves, huntsman and Snow White lying across seven tiny beds. Sunshine and Raine turn to Raquel when they see her photo, but Raquel stays in her seat looking sulky.

The costumes are good. No kid made them, but they're good.

"It's not fair!" Leila whispers in my ear. "They had adult help."

The acting coach struggles back to his seat, congratulating the children who were wearing the costumes. He shakes hands with the tall skinny girl who played the queen and the dark-haired boy, sitting beside her, who played the huntsman. He high-fives with the Seven Dwarves who start singing, "Hi, ho, hi, ho, it's off to work we go." Mr. Actor dramatically puts one finger to his lips, puts his other hand out to the side and uses his whole body to mime "Shhhh!" Then takes his seat, giving Raquel a thumbs up. She gives him a half-hearted smile and slumps down in her chair.

"What's up with 'You-haven't-got-a-hope-of-winning-without-me'?" I murmur.

"Best Music this year goes to..." Mr. Booming Voice continues then fumbles with another envelope.

I know this one won't be ours. I didn't really think about music apart from the Monster Mash at the Palace Ball.

"Dominic Drummond Drama for their film, *The Seven Dwarves Meet Snow White.*"

Mr. Actor's mouth drops open and he brings both of his hands to his cheeks. There's a montage of dramatic music showing the queen approaching the mirror, the huntsman running through some trees and then the familiar dwarf song from the Disney film. The pink shirts sing at the top of their voices as their leader pushes another child onto the stage to collect the prize. Dad starts whistling so I shoot him an evil look.

It's Robyn's turn. "Best Cinematography goes to... Dominic Drummond Drama for *The Seven Dwarves Meet Snow White.*"

Robyn didn't even look at the card before announcing the winner. More clips appear on the screen, more congratulations given, more fake surprise on Mr. Actor's face. *Why are we here? It's all about Mr. Actor and his pink stars. And what is going on with Raquel? She is the only one not celebrating. So far we've only seen her costume, nothing else. This is weird.*

"Best animation for the year goes to..." Mr. Booming Voice announces whilst opening the envelope.

"Surely, they can't have won this as well," I whisper to Leila, who giggles quietly.

"Giorgos Papadopoulos for his film *Jack and the Beanstalk.*"

There is some polite applause as a small boy wearing glasses stands near the back of the auditorium and makes his way to the front.

"George!" I gasp.

"I taught him how to animate in Computer Club," Ivan says, sounding outraged. "And now he's beaten me."

"Well done, George. I didn't know you had entered," Mr. Phillips says as the boy walks down the aisle. Mr. Richardson looks at my teacher as if he is asking whether he should know this child.

"He's in my class and your Computer Club," Mr. Phillips explains.

Mr. Richardson starts clapping much louder and sits bolt upright as if this success is somehow his award.

A Lego farm is built, brick by brick, in stop-motion animation as the title of George's film appears on the screen. Everything is Lego: Jack, the cow, his mother, the beans, the beanstalk, even the axe.

"This must have taken him days and days to make!" I say, astonished.

"Did you know about this?" I ask Ivan, who shakes his head.

"Our next award is for Best Editor," Robyn announces, and I swing my head back to face the stage. "The unsung hero of the film industry takes all the work recorded and somehow creates a story that we can all enjoy."

There is a pause while she struggles with the envelope. I cross my fingers and close my eyes tightly.

"This year's winner is... Ivan V..." Robyn continues.

"Vladivenski!" I shout. "Ivan that's you!"

"For the film, *Cinderella*," Robyn concludes, smiling in our direction.

Leila, Ben, Sunshine, Raine and I jump out of our seats and turn to see Ivan hugging his mom and dad. The twins quickly sit down when Raquel gives them an evil look but in the *Cinderella* area, we celebrate.

"Let's go, Ivan, let's go, toot, toot," I sing. Ben and Leila join in, but Mrs. Choudhury stops us with a look.

Ivan struggles to the aisle, shaking Mr. Richardson's hand as he passes and getting a firm pat on the back from Mr. Phillips, whose eyes are glistening.

He looks small on stage as he shakes hands with Mr. Booming Voice and takes the cup. Then Robyn says something to him. We can't hear it over the noise of our voices and the audience's applause, but Ivan's face goes red as he turns to the screen.

My hand-drawn bubble writing comes up on the big screen, *Cinderella*. My film is going to be shown here, in public. A warm feeling gushes inside me, my fingers tingle and I sit up quickly so I can see.

They play clips of Sunshine and Raine ordering me about, then the Khan Academy animation of the palace trumpeters, quickly followed by an image of the front page of the *Once Upon a Times* newspaper announcing that a Grand Ball will be held at the palace. There's my dad in his black leathers announcing, "An invitation from the palace," with the twins running out of the house to take it, cut to a picture of the invitation, written in my best writing, then Sunshine and Raine leaving for the ball and appearing in their First Communion dresses at the Halloween Dance. There's an invitation to the wedding of the prince and Cinderella, and the clips pause on my sign saying 'The End.'

I slump back in my chair. *We did it! We actually won a prize!* The audience is clapping politely as Ivan returns with his cup and a gift certificate for a place at Spring Break Film Camp.

"Look Maddie, look what I won!" Ivan says, leaning over my shoulder.

"Cool," I reply, feeling a little bit jealous that Ivan won the prize when the film was my idea.

"This year we have a new award for Best Movie Action," Mr. Booming Voice announces. "One of our sponsors, All Action Inc. are generously giving away ten classes at their academy, where our winner can learn some professional stunt skills such as hand-to-hand combat, sword fighting and horseback archery."

There's a long pause as the envelope is opened. I hold my breath and cross my fingers on both hands. Leila leans towards me and Ivan crouches on the floor behind my seat. *If I win this, I will always do my homework and never pick at a scab again,* I offer to the Universe.

"Our first award for Movie Action goes to Madeleine Moore for the film *Cinderella*."

"What?!" I shout.

Leila pushes and Ivan pulls me to my feet. My

stomach feels as if it has dropped to the floor and bounced back into my mouth. Mom and Dad are half hugging and half pulling me towards the end of the row. Mr. Richardson is smiling and shaking his head. Mr. Phillips is laughing so hard there are tears coming from his eyes.

My legs don't want to work, but somehow I make it to the stage and get to shake hands with Robyn! Mr. Booming Voice steps away from the microphone, congratulates me, turns my body towards the screen and holds my shoulders so I have to stay and watch.

There on the big screen is my fall from the roof — the audience gasps — Dad's wheelie — the audience cheers — Leila hovering mid-air and descending, frame by frame in slow motion — there's a long "oh" from the audience — my stair fall — the audience draws in its breath through gritted teeth — and the pumpkin carriage racing down the road.

"Way to go Maddie!" Mr. Phillips shouts and everyone laughs.

The screen then freezes on a picture of me flying through the air just before I landed in Mrs. Green's pile of leaves. There are claps and cheers from all over the theatre. Mom and Dad hug each other. The sea of pink is copying the way my arms are stretched out into thin air like a flying superhero. Leila, Ben and Ivan are jumping up and down. Even Mrs. Choudhury and Mr. Richardson are smiling and clapping.

If I was to drop dead right now, I would have every-thing I ever wanted in the world. Everyone looks happy for me. Well, everyone except Raquel whose evil look doesn't even stop the twins looking thrilled for me. She is the only person who's not clapping or cheering, and for once, I don't care.

I don't know how I got back to my seat, but once there I sit and stare at my cup and gift certificate. There are things happening around me, more awards, more clap-ping, more pink squeals, but I just sit. There is a bubble of joy around me that is so cozy, warm and sweet that I never want to move again. *What is this feeling?* There is stillness inside me. No rushing ideas. No urge to jump up. Just a warm glow like hot chocolate and hugs, but it's all me. *Oh, I could definitely do this all over again!*

"In our mind, you are all winners," Mr. Booming Voice brings me back to the ceremony. "But our last award tonight is for The Young Filmmaker of the Year's Best Film."

"And the winner is...the fractured fairy tale," Robyn takes over. "*The Seven Dwarves Meet Snow White.*"

The Pink Sea scream, Mr. Actor pretends to faint and Raquel's mother gives her an enormous hug. Mom nudges my side and I join in the clapping.

There's some dramatic music as the dwarves mine for jewels in a dark cave. There are soldiers standing guard, giving orders to work harder, and refusing to let them stop for water or food. Then there's a cut to the queen wearing a dress covered in jewels, looking in the mirror and asking, "Mirror, mirror on the wall, who is the fairest of them all?"

Of course, the mirror replies that the queen is the fairest and she orders more jewels. Back to the dwarves, one tries to escape but is caught by the huntsman and dragged before the queen who puts a price on his head "Ten rubies as red as my lips, twelve sapphires as blue as my eyes, fifty diamonds to match my sparkling wit and his weight in gold must be brought to me or he dies at sunset."

The audience boos then laughs and we see the six remaining dwarves rescuing the prisoner and climbing into barrels to escape.

"That's come straight from *The Hobbit*," Ivan whispers in my ear. "Your ideas are far better."

"And I bet they are not even in there," I add as the barrels float down a river.

"I should hope not," Mrs. Choudhury says as the dwarves climb out of their barrels on dry land and look around a beautiful field of wild flowers.

"Where's Raquel's part?" Leila asks.

I shrug and look across the audience. Raquel's mom is leaning over towards her and whispering intensely. "You're not the only one wondering," I say, nodding in Raquel's direction.

The queen is back on the screen demanding that the dwarves are caught and that the huntsman bring her a fox and some rabbits for a new coat.

"Now it's *101 Dalmatians*," Ivan comments.

Cut to the dwarves singing "Hi, ho, hi, ho" as they build a new home. Several young children dressed as rabbits arrive, looking for protection from the queen, which the dwarves promise to give them.

Back at the palace, the huntsman presents the queen with a fox fur stole with the head and feet still attached.

"Err, gross!" I whisper, screwing up my face.

"Mirror, mirror on the wall, who is the fairest of them all?" the queen asks.

"There is one with skin as white as snow, lips as red as rubies, they call her Snow White. She is the fairest in the land," the mirror replies.

The queen goes into a rage and smashes the mirror, watched by a mouse. *Wow, I can see why she won best actress. She's really good and VERY scary.*

The mouse tells a squirrel, the squirrel tells a badger, the badger tells a bird and the bird flies to the dwarves' cottage and tells them of the danger Snow White is in.

"Bring her here and we will protect her," one of the dwarves decides.

Then the film cuts to Snow White lying asleep on the dwarves' beds, surrounded by the mouse, squirrel, badger, bird and the Seven Dwarves.

"She'll be safe with us," claims the leader of the dwarves and 'The End' appears on the screen.

"That's it?!" I gasp as everyone applauds. "Raquel didn't even speak."

Mr. Booming Voice moves back to the microphone. "Thank you all for coming to the Tenth Young Filmmaker of the Year Awards. We hope to see you back here next year with the new theme, *It was a Dark and Stormy Night.*"

The lights come on and people start putting on their coats and moving to the doors. Winners are being congratulated. Others are being comforted.

"How about a celebratory ice cream for the Best Editor and Best Movie Action," Dad suggests as we leave.

"Can I invite the Best Animator?" Ivan asks, pushing through the crowd to reach George.

"And I'm going to see if the twins can join us," I say,

grabbing Leila's hand. "Sunshine, Raine... we're going to DQ to celebrate. Want to join us?"

"We've been invited to the 3D Acting for Life after-show party," Sunshine says sounding disappointed.

"I don't think it will be much fun," Raine adds, looking at Raquel.

"One scene, that's it! I told my friends that you were Snow White," Raquel's mom says, going red in the face.

"I was Snow White," Raquel cries.

"I even found an agent who asked me to send a copy of the movie. I can't send her that! All that money on classes and costumes and you didn't even speak!" Raquel's mom rages.

I stand frozen to the spot, watching Raquel's crumpling face. *Wow! Her mom is harsh.*

"Come on," Leila says, pulling me away.

"See you at school," I shout to the twins as I run up to our group and show my cup and prize to everyone.

I look back towards Raquel. Her mother turns away from my enemy, who's trying hard to stop crying. Sunshine and Raine put their arms around her. I almost feel sorry for her.

"Maybe you could invite her to be part of your next movie," Mom suggests, putting her arm around me and moving the group to the door.

"Now, about my next movie," I shout. "I have an idea!"

ABOUT THE AUTHOR

Sonia Garrett was born in England, moved to California when she was three weeks old, went to school in Australia, and spent most of her adult life in England where she graduated from the University of East Anglia with a BA (Hons) in Drama and English. She is always up for an adventure and has worked as a dancer, clown, actor, and teacher. She owned a Gymboree Play and Music franchise, and now seems to have settled down to being a Mom, Montessori Teacher, storyteller and writer.

She lives in the gentle chaos of books, outdoor paraphernalia, cooking ingredients and gardening equipment in Vancouver, Canada with her stunt performer/co-ordinator husband, Rich, and their daughter, Jacquie.

To connect with Sonia please visit

www.soniagarrett.com

sonia@soniagarrett.com

Made in the USA
Middletown, DE
01 December 2020